Love and the Stranger and all the forever things

Love and the Stranger and all the forever things

by Kyle Gougeon

ISBN:9798315090540

Cover art credit to Mrs. Tammy Gougeon

Other works by Kyle Gougeon:

Love and Cupid and all the sultry things

Love and the Muses and all the luscious things

For Tammy, you are always more than I can ever dream

I know I will one day forget the Stranger. I know Love will one day forgive the Stranger. We are in the slow and the caution, we are in the grip of becoming whole again. Our memories will be clean. Our memories will be ours. We will know the wash in the softer corners of the night, we will know the wash in the most delicate fingers of the day. The stolen harmony is on our breath, we never fell through our own hands. We were never meant to be his possessions. We were never meant for his fires. We became the Stranger's unexpected pleasure, an unexpected keep.

To think of him is a poison, to acknowledge him is surrender. And I know to speak with him is suffocation. I have laid before and within and beyond the Stranger's madness. I know the cost and I know the promise, I know the revelry and the dreams lost. I know the fall through the kaleidoscope does not match the rise.

If his words were indeed words at all, they fall like scrapings, they echo like a silent nightmare. And when I find the forgiveness, perhaps I will find the belief my skin will lose the crawl from his touch. I lay on my back in this night's deepest shade and sense its cool shallow and hollow all around me. I listen to Love sleeping beside me. I try to forgive myself for feeling the scratch he made. I try to forgive myself for remembering the punctures, I barely felt the stink of his callouses.

There was something I wanted to tell you, there was something that escaped any mind or mood I may have had. I thought it was important enough to allow myself the company of the Stranger. There were words I believed forever would not allow. I tell myself that in your sleep, you have heard all I wished to say, and you understand.

The dark cleverness of the Stranger allows him to elude time and space. He was the last rain of sand upon the universe, he was the empty, the fill, the bridge between past and present. He had no strength and no direction. His steps were meant to pass unnoticed. He was to be unnamed and breathless and serve no other purpose. The universe could not deny him once he stood. He was to exist no longer than his brief and lonely song. The Stranger was created to be a twist and a turn and a longing, and then he was to be forgotten. That was the universe's cold and cruel success. He was a mistake, a misfortune, a beginning without an end.

I cough deep and loud into midnight, into a hand you have since reclaimed. A hand you brought home. We are a page beyond within a book I dreamed. We are a survival we hope is beyond the reach. There were promises I wanted to make.

And the Stranger was forgotten, he was set free into a prison, he was forgotten and left to wonder and hunger. He became curious, he began to learn. He did not suffer, he did not disappear, he began to glow as he watched from afar, as he watched from outside, peering through the doors and windows the world created. He listened to the bags of secrets the world did not think it needed to hide. He loomed in the shadows the world could not see through.

The Stranger smiled first, he smiled after and behind. He was forgotten. Forgotten was his illness, his weakness, until it became his reason. Forgotten became his warmth and his food and his drink. Roads were laid and he walked through the mud, bridges were raised and he walked through the rivers. Towns were formed and nobody spoke his name or knew his face.

Beauty was defined and he tore himself blind. Devotion was spoken and he tore himself deaf. He should not have been more than a brief chill of an enchanting evening, or a brief swallow against the most lovely words ever spoken.

He was a promise no one was supposed to speak. He was ambition never meant for light. He was born, knowing how to walk. He walked through the most insignificant times of the rolling events we all chose to ignore and take no interest in. He walked and gathered all and everything in his pockets, he gathered them as charms and chains. He concealed them all in his pockets, as chains and charms. He was timid at first, before discovering he could bleed and ease through crowds the same as he could clouds.

8

He could fly with the birds and even sing with them, or choke them. He could rise and whisper like trees, and even sing with them, or burn with them. He discovered the endless possibilities of invisibility.

And long before I met the Stranger, all I wanted was to give you a dream.

The Stranger walked until someone finally spoke his name. His name was to be spoken once and then forgotten. It became his first perfect madness. The walk became the hunt, the hunt became the exquisite joy. The joy became the motive, the motive became the revenge. The walk became the dance, the dance became a story, the story was ripped from me and draped wet around his neck and soft in his teeth.

My Love, you stir at my side, and I toss and long and clench, like I remember my hunger. I was going to whisper about the forever things that roll across my bones, I was going to whisper about the forever things that fall like lace across my eyes.

The Stranger's chains and charms became snakes in the grass and snakes in the gardens. He awoke one day, long before he and I met, and his smile licked into his eyes. He put his fingers into the soup, and then he plunged his face into it. I run a finger across your long hip, I stop myself from speaking into the night. He is lurking, in the goodness, he is trying to put his taste into the meat, he has his feet in the gravy.

The romantic in me believes he discovered us during a windswept night. We had nothing to cling to or long for, except everything we believed in. We were hooked to the mountaintops, and stuffed and swollen and wedged deep, there was a new happiness. We were in a happiness that is long and thick as it dripped through the boundaries. It had only been a few years, and my eyes were still adjusting to it. Our tongues were acquiring the taste, our arms and legs were becoming familiar. The romantic in me believes the Stranger appeared somewhere between unseen and unheard and unfelt. He was just beyond the bliss. He was just beyond the truth.

The romantic in me believes all the windows and the doors were closed, our mouths were past comfort and our heads were leading to dreams. He must have appeared just beyond the vibrant and the excruciating pleasure and the colors and the simplicity. The Stranger must have paused his journey, he heard us like lovers, he looked upon us like dogs. He felt a stab of the unknown, a moment passing the eyes of delight. The romantic in me believes we could not feel him stirring the waves, we couldn't hear him over the rain, we didn't sense him through the currents, we never invited him in.

The romantic in me believes I tried to protect us, I rose and fell, and then you tried to protect us, and I distracted you with a kiss. We were lost in the boil, lost hard in the lovesavage, the day had already dripped into darkness and we were unsuspecting. We were so longwet our other eyes never saw him coming. My wants and haves were so tight in that delicious wrap, I never insisted upon bringing the covers up high. I sensed the chill and never brought our bed to cover our necks. I never brought you tight and closer than you could possibly be.

And to write about the Stranger is to risk another accidental swim through his hourglass. His perfect chaos is in his walk and his speak, his blend of the now and the then and the when. He leaves us fighting and swimming against the sands. I will have to risk the accidental trilogy that becomes and ends with Love and the Stranger and the forever things.

We paid the final forgotten price on a Wednesday, and found ourselves surrendering to the charms on a Thursday. And that is where we thought we left it, never following the heels of the unknown or the unheld. Our laughs were meant to exist in the soft and in the appetite. The charms will always be mirrored by the chains, their length and girth stretch side by side. In perfect times, they rule the grass and the gardens equally, in harmony. We are forever found, and we are forever lost, between the demands of the charms and the chains. The steady, heavy charms, and the unpredictable chains. The universe kicks its magic off its feet, when the charms and the chains stretch like two snakes and coexist.

I will relive the accidental trilogy with the Narrator's words and discover I have the Narrator's eyes, the new and the used and old and those that are still waiting. The bells were ringing, I still hear them. Love had my heart within her own gentle heart. The days were crashing one upon the next, they were moving aside to be replaced and abandoned. I hear them as well. To speak of the Stranger is to forget all the maps and allow him into your veins. He has no desire for time or coherence. Once he has been heard, he has already been felt, he has choked out the indifference and choked free the subtle and the normal. The past becomes the enemy you embrace as a friend, the present loses its purpose and swallows its own belly to become the next instant. The future leaves to wash itself and returns as a ghost and becomes a flash behind the lightning. The universe should have awakened, it should have panicked, it should have rustled and rattled. We should have been warned when the Stranger's eyes found our door. Neither of us were prepared for the unbecoming, the unnatural.

11

I can't remember when we saw the darkness coming, the Stranger may have already taken our eyes. I don't remember when we ran or if we even tried to run away. I can't remember when the pale became the normal, I can't remember the struggle or the return. Or if the world leapt at the heave of the forever things.

I think I remember I wanted the careless burn of a writer's pen to tell you all the things I could not. I wanted to tell you of the forever things. You did not bring the sun to rise, it came upon legs of its own. And now here are your eyes, here is your smile, here is your press. Here is your comfort, here is your desire. I am remembering the man I promised to be. My lips are working themselves free from a word and a twist, my heart is growing into a pile. The fires within are the fires we reach. And I love you more than the words I can find. My hands grow larger than what we are dealt, and grow larger than what we can dream. They grow soft and gentle at your face. They will always risk the grip, they will always grow humble at your embrace, and ask more and more.

My hand will seek your slightest touch and your firmest grip, it will long for the longest, the first and the next and the last. I love how we never resist. I love how you talk like a sultry angel and want like a luscious promise. I feel everything you feel, I have escaped everything you have escaped.

If we keep our footing and our thunder, we will remain within the fences and the lines. If we keep our wits, we will outlast the lighting and the impossible. We oil our hearts beneath the moonlight, we water our hearts beneath the covers. We chase each other through the night. My Love, we need only speak the truth out on the grass and within these aching walls. When the pleasures become immeasurable, once they stop showing their teeth and singing their songs, once they have surrendered their cages and they are finding their tidy corners. We are closer to the forever things. When the past no longer shows its belly and shows its lips, when it finds us too difficult to manage, when it has crashed through its ceiling and discovered its clouds. We are closer to the forever things.

Two souls have clasped into one, one lovetrapped, lovedreamed, one that has waited so long it has forgotten its birthday. One soul and the charms and the chains become three. One for the discovery, one for the test, and one for the realization. When Love and Leo become us. There is all which waited within a dream, there is all which waited in the dirt. And the next will always offer us the opportunity to board the wrong train. My Love, we whisper unspeakable truths, we hold untouchable truths.

While I wear the face of the Narrator, I would warn against wisdom, I would suffer as the wise. I would warn against the common and suffer as the nearly pure. I would warn against ambition that is dressed in riches, I would dance as the dreamers. I would warn curiosity sees the holes in the quilt, and I would suffer the warm.

The Stranger still breathes his long exhale into the beginning of this story. It is his fondness for the splinters he places within the present and past. It is his secret. It is the way he puts the powder on us, and holds us like a crust of bread. It is the way he opens his mouth like a vacuum and then a tornado. He is the shiver from yesterday, and the mine to walk across today. Our journey with him was brief, then complete, then never ending.

BEFORE

We sense the changing of the seasons, it is like a new voice in the room. Our steps lead our eyes outside. Fall has come, fall has disobeyed the calendar. She has arrived perhaps only to visit, it is too early to take her blossomed daughters home. They have had the entirety of spring and summer to be with us, grow with us, teach us, dance with us. It is too early to go home. Some still have new growth, some have dew. Fall has her fingers just beyond the vision of the world, I have some of my fingers at Love's cheek and I kiss her good morning.

'I love this,' she says. Because what has grown never truly wilts or fades. It does not surrender, it maintains its place. The colors will stagger away and we will leave a path for their return. This is a small push before fall arrives. Love and I know she betrays her own name. She is a rise and a comfortable walk. The sun will light differently, relaxing and no longer reaching above the trees. The temperatures will cool and all that treated us and soothed us with magnificent tones and colors will soon lay upon the ground. It is all part of the natural evolution. The days before the slow vanishing, the days before waiting for the return of spring.

This is the next pool Love and I calmly enter, this is the next current we lay within. It is nearly Fall and it is time to relax with autumn speak and autumn wishes. This is just another day in the long enchantment, a day we need not pursue, a time we do not follow or trap. I know every reason why our happiness will be longer than Love's hair. This is just another morning that is content to have only a gentle song. This is a day returned from the lost, recovered from the stolen. Were it not so peaceful, it could be considered a reward.

Love has abandoned her coffee and is drifting through the yard and spreading her whispers and her ways. I know enough to

14

walk among them and around them, I know enough to be careful. These are not the charms, these will lift me from the ground.

It is a beautiful day to be in love with an angel, it is a beautiful day to admire the pure workings of a pure soul. It would not be a show of strength, it would not be a sacrifice, it would not be endurance or weakness, to say I would trade all my haves and my wants, all that I have been and all that I have learned, to see her face. I want to give her everything, and she smiles, because this is all she wants. Here I will stand, between the before and the forever. The largest man I have within me happily crumbles into the magic and the shade, as she blows me a kiss.

Her eyes say, 'My Leo,' and I am once again the boy who knew her, I am once again the boy who loved her. Those old roads, the ones that found us, the ones that saved us, they have become worn and faded, they have been redirected and lost and their dirt silenced. Those old skies, the ones that watched us, the ones that helped us hide, they have rolled and moved on and rest above the forever pastures. We have had them before, all the charms and the chains, we have no need for them now. Love comes back to find the relief of my shoulders. She smiles and finds the white in my whiskers, out here in the sunlight. I was once that boy before I became her man of all seasons.

I want to tell her things my morning notes fail to capture. I want to tell her the boil will outlast even the burn, it will outlast the kettle. The boil will outlast the meat and the juice and the spices. It will outlast the fires and even the hands that created it. One day it will still be us.

Before the boil and beyond the boil, it will be just us. In the pleasure and the truth, in the fairness and the simplicity. Our backs will ache from the fever's long refusal to break, our skin will wrinkle with it, our eyes will learn new trances and greetings, our ears will forget old words. Forever is never a goodbye. We are Love and Leo, a hand in a hand, a kiss at a mouth, a heart at a rib, a pull at a want, an oath to a promise. We are the souls that can not stop chasing the lovewet.

At the back of my throat I know I will love you more, in front of every eye and doubt, every longing and wandering eye, I will always love you in the moment. In our moment. We will always recognize whichever face it chooses to wear. We stand before forever and it will never come between us.

The gates of a paradise have become unlocked and we are here in it. The golds and the oranges, the reds and the purples are throwing themselves against the trees. They are newly arriving, and I sense a brief crisp in the air. I feel a slight pause and a concern, and I will blame it on yesterday. Because winter is waiting and fall is here and nothing is wrong. I want the quiet to know this can be a place for its waves, I want the quiet to know we will lay down in it, it can surround us.

Love is again dancing among the charms, and they are dancing with her. They are the charms that soothe, the charms that bind. The charms that whisper in a soft sensual ruin and delight. The charms feed and fill the spaces so we need no doors or walls. These are the charms that can not speak cold or alone. These are the charms before the dark finds its voice. The charms bring their light and hang the feeders so the angels might come and see our callouses and see what we have done. They can taste our reunion and our redemption. The angels have busy, worrisome minutes, they fly into clouds and promise they will return before they disappear. They come and go above the pull of the chains before they rise and join all of the eyes in the stars.

The chains are dressed long with links and not meant to be ours today. The links lay in wait and want, hungry for the one before and hungry for the one that is next. Each link can be for any and each and all. One for the past, one for injustice, one for disappointment and one for uncertainty. A link for you for to forget and another I will try not to remember. We will avoid them as they howl and others wait like sunshine or shadow. We will avoid them today, as they begin to coil and roll like shivers and lay straight like innocence. The chains and charms are forever, but they are never intertwined.

I don't know why they choose to lay before us, on such a fine swollen day. We will treat them like dogs with no gained attention or affection. Even those which may be ours will have no weight or voice today.

There are the charms Love and I share, those we have grown and those we shelter, and those which set us free. And the chains can not wrap us in boxes, they can't bring the lurch of the land or the lunge of the sea. They are lost mud from lost pasts. Before forever. The chains fall into pieces. Love's chains can not be heard above the music, my chains can not find the pace of the walk.

Today has become a soaking fire of the forever things, today has become a resting windstorm of the forever things. Love and I have grown weightless with them. Today is without limits, without hours, it is without fatigue and without a tongue. It is a day no one will possess. Today is the thin crack between life and dream. Between want and have. Today is the line, the hair, the whisper between more and most.

The forever things are once again unearthed and freed, they fall like rain, they come without demands and mania. They are crawling and standing and learning to walk. The forever things have no memories, each is new and each is perfection. Each is left to be a stone forgotten, a stone for the next to lay upon, a stone to rise into an impossible mountain. The forever things learn to speak and learn to sing and learn to run and learn to heal. They create satisfaction dreams and ambition paths. Theirs is to call and never be called. Theirs is to possess and never be possessed. Theirs is to touch and never be touched.

If there were ever a day I could be more than a narrator, if I could be a writer to describe what my eyes can see. My eyes serve my heart and my heart is taken and deliciously spoken for. She has never been more gorgeous, not even the day my world was turned on its side. I have never been so complete and hungry. She is the truth at my skin, the breath at my lips.

I ache when she finds me, dreaming among the living. She comes with a seek and never escapes my hands, she searches their longing and understands they can't breathe without her. She gives herself to them when they are red with the labor of the day and deep with the ease of the evening. And they surrender to her, promising there is nothing else.

If there was a voice so bold to carry the melody of the pledge. I am fearless when I stand beside her, I am fearless when I kneel before her. If there were courageous and undemanding words. I will find her through the cold, I will find her through the secret and the peace. I will find her through any fear, through the reach and the take, I will find her more and always.

If I could explain the reward and the wishes of the forever things. If I could share this moment and how it trembles as it becomes. Love found me before the broken roads we traveled, she found me before I became unwilling to escape. I stand proud, I have her hairs and feathers upon me and all around me. To reach for a kiss is to take another step, to step is to scream into the fall, to scream is to announce it without a single breath of doubt. To breathe is to discover and to embrace it. To embrace it is not remember the crushed man I was before the fast slick forever.

I absolutely adored Love before the forever reward, the forever worth and the forever joy. The patience we feel for this day will last until the night, before the hammering longing comes into my walk, before it comes into my bones, before I take her hand in the moonlight. She is the reason, I feel it standing close beside her. I want her to say 'My Leo' so I can hear it as though it were the first time.

I want to surprise her and tease her, release her and be buried beneath her. We can't pretend we didn't feel the universe drop to its knees when we met. We can't pretend there aren't flavors and promises we have not tasted before. My Love, here in another of our moments within all the forever things, I wish I could tell you I can't pretend I haven't been possessed, so carefully possessed, so emphatically possessed. I have been gloriously chewed, I have been sensually eaten, I am happily devoured.

We have long outlasted the pull of the fool's burn. We were innocent before we were lovers, we are innocent now. The universe can't find its excuses before it speaks, it can't explain the reasons why forever did not come before waiting. Why wanting came before us. We never let go. We never weakened before our final stand. Before the honey came, before the wounds were never spelled and never spoken of. We would never want in this swirling have.

I carelessly offer it before the universe, somewhere beyond the charms and the chains, it is listening. Love and I have a feel and a savor, we have a share and a promise, a sweetness that escapes the candy and a strength that escapes the dark. Our passion can outrun the fever and its cure. I carelessly speak and the edges begin racing towards us. I am blind, my hands are blind against her cheek in the afternoon, they are blind in her hair in the evening. My heart speaks it out into the universe. Beyond the volumes I have narrated to her, I want to give her the elusive words I feel are out there, I want to give her something she has never seen.

Before the forgiveness and the forgetting must come the story of the days and nights and all we wish to believe never happened. There was an instant of a strange feeling of a dry violence, a catastrophe looming. An innocent mistake is made before there can be redemption. There was pure before the filth, pure walked into the noise, the noise walked with no direction until it came upon the calm. I try to remember if our eyes opened before we fell to crawl.

My Love, you are my pleasure, you are the presence, I need to be about your knees and ankles. I need to tell you what I see. I need your shoulders strong above my head, I need the last to be everlasting. I need the first to return to the front of the line. I need your softness to grip me, I need the middle of this afternoon to maintain its trust.

I wish to find the words to say it, all that I feel. The truth suffers no curiosity, it suffers no hesitation. That single chance we boldly took is our ever after, we taste it every day. If I could lose the voice of the narrator struggle through a writer's simple words. We walked a road people had forgotten, the gods had forgotten, time and the world had long forgotten. We walked a road and I saw your sweet face. And then there was the first and last time I ever asked for your hand, and every lifetime between.

Forgive my innocence and I will forgive yours, forgive me of all the crimes I never committed and I will forgive you. We do not bend or beg for the forever things, they are seeping into all we do, all we know. They call like the spoon we feed from, they call like the dish we sleep in. They are hooked around our necks, they are the pulse, the pine and the give, the want and the have. They are the salt and the warmth, they are the impossible that feels so easy.

For a moment I lose the weight, only to find it again upon my shoulders. And if I could abandon the legs of the narrator, I would run from this anxious, accidental trilogy. There was nothing but warmth in the days. But my path collided with the Stranger, so our path collided with the Stranger. It is difficult to say which days will be healed, which days will be lived, and which days will be forgotten. I can't honestly say we are here, and now, for all of this could be another cruelty.

The Stranger placed a twist within time. He laughed when yesterday was choking today, he laughed harder when tomorrow stumbled into the chaotic fight. I knew he could not simply snap his fingers and change day into night. But I saw him do it. There was so much he claimed was impossible and I witnessed it to be possible. He found the insides of the deep songs, he found the insides of the silent fires. The Stranger was and is and can be.

Love and I have been in the leaves, we have been in the arms and the embraces of the branches. We have inventoried all which spring and summer have now abandoned, we have cultivated all which will return and never be lost or forgotten. The long heated afternoons of July and August suddenly become a gentle spray. We join and rejoin, time and again. Labor and lunch, labor and a pause, labor and kiss, labor and a rest. The dramatic is but the simple and the comfortable. All the vibrance, their songs and their hues, their hums and tones, their voices have not left us. Some are fading, some are weeping and some remain proud in the cooling air.

Everything has its season, everything knows the strikes of Time. Everything knows her restless, nurturing, working hands. I wonder what seasons we have had, and all the seasons which await. What we don't fully remember remains in our hearts, and our souls have a language to speak of it. Troubles may lurk and troubles may seek, but they have no chairs or bedding here.

Love awakens my purest senses. I watch her drift around the patio, smelling each bloom that refuses to sleep. Life can be this simple. The chains lay silently beneath the dimming day. The charms are about like fishermen's lines. I don't know how the seasons may whisper or plan. I look down into my own hands and see those which seek the forever things. In my own reflection I can clearly see that which was but hints of gray have come with courage and numbers and covered my face. I am long into that season. But Love is still barefoot at this late hour of the afternoon and there is youth and I am still upon the best of my legs.

We should dream tonight, my Love, and I know we will. The world will find a fold to keep just us two. We will dream, when the plates are finished, when the pots and pans are gone. When the face of the clock is covered and our room has the only remaining voice. We can dream and play in the clouds for a short while, we can dance with tomorrow, we can always dance with tomorrow. We can whisper the secrets lovers have already shared and never tire of hearing. We can walk along the path that little boy and that little girl knew, before their small hands grew into our grasp.

Love's face finds its way to my chest. 'I love you more,' she says. For a moment I am off balance, but I give her my best and most famous kiss. Above the silence I tell myself we do not need the boredom of perfection. It is us, it is she and I, in this day and night, as we dressed and will undress. As the sand rushes down, we are the thick syrup, we are the soft against the edges, we are the certainty above the questions. We are the raft upon the river, a sigh against the neck, a shoulder to receive a thigh, a hand that doesn't need to search the dark.

Love's eyes are removed from a shadow and return to blue in the light, and oh how my mouth works to speak. I would walk with a narrator's foot and a writer's hand without a worry. I clumsily lay it out in the grass for the universe to grasp. I would suffer so she never will. I want to give her all she has never had. We have no need to find our place, we have been found. We have all the markings braised between young and hopelessly hopeful, and older and dangerously certain. The markings are upon her back and across my chest. There is one at her cheek and one upon my chin. They are in our hands and in our words. The beauty and the imperfection of the forever things. The promise of the forever things.

And their soothing cries. I don't want to stand and wait for those electric nights. We don't pay the cost of waiting. Half of humanity may lay on its belly in struggle, and we may struggle as well, but we will not suffer the wait. I want to come a little closer and tell her things I know I have not yet said. I want to walk along with her a little farther because there is nowhere else I'd rather be. Shh, you can turn down the lights, I am already home. There are words and gazes and longings that can only exist to cross pillows and her hair. There are touches that can only be felt with fingers and touches felt without fingers. I am growing impatient for the day's drag into this night. Tonight, it's tonight I seek, my thirst won't dry, I have visions of unpracticed dances. I have visions of the comets we will ride. It is too late to speak of this morning, and this afternoon will not drop its hands. It is too early to speak of the memories of tonight. We are in the quicksand and there is nothing more to want.

We speak in lovetense, with a lovetease, we flex in the tension, we are gripped and released. We speak neither past or future, but with the dirty words of contentment and truths. Bound and freed, we feel every delicious rub. To be a writer and not a narrator, to bring light to the taste of her lips, to make it eternal. To share the scent and the feel and the escape of the forever things. I want the world to run with the weight of the forever things, I want the world to run with the ruin of the forever things. She knows where my eyes have been and what they have seen, and she loves me. We know the bells that rang through the lives before, the ones we didn't deserve, the ones where we stood proud and didn't belong. We know the dances we churned through, before the music ended and before it began.

This love tale was never laid before us, never gifted as a calm, never loaned as a cure, never stolen as a right. This love tale took us and shook us like a hurricane. We don't want to resurface, we don't want to recover. This soft, simple unbending ease, it is unending. The lightness and darkness we knew before, the screams that drowned out the dreams. Those feelings and visions are not forgotten, they have ceased to be. They were to live as a struck match. Those hard pasts are gone and as unreachable as the last wind.

I would skip the next breath to bring this night closer. I feel the reach and the gaze of tonight. I want its roast, I want its touch, I want to lay in the pieces of the morning. My Love has had action and intention all day, and I have felt motionless, losing the piles of minutes and hours. The ache is in my throat, the want has its hands on the side of my face. 'My sweet Leo,' she says. I was a writer before I was a narrator. I knew the slow suggestive slide of the writer before the hills to climb as a narrator. If I could gather and speak the words of this moment.

We have little memory of the mirrors that once stared at us, we can't picture the faces they had. We can't remember what was said, before I heard her voice and she heard mine. We can't remember what we saw before our eyes met in the daylight, I don't remember having any vision at all before our eyes met in the night. The paths which possessed our steps no longer have names. The fear which suffocated our freedom no longer has heat. That which was before and never again.

She and I tirelessly writhe in the lover's battle. It is a war of perfection, a war of consumption. There is not an enemy to be found, there is not a blow to be struck. There was a beginning and no end. There is only the faith, there is us and ours and all the rest. Love and Leo can be held within a single touch or kiss. All the rest fills and consumes the world. The enormity of the forever things may rest across the shoulders of a grain of sand and be carried by its legs. The forever things are an experience and not a possession.

Our private whispers are galloping around the yard, they are crawling over the roof and begging the walls not to bend. I believe there was a cold, before what I know now, before this moment. I believe there was an empty, before this always. My Love will bring her heart and soul to me, she will bring her shoulders and elbows and knees to me. She will bring her sense to me. She will ask about my tears, I have never cried with such joy. She has made me man enough to weep and never cry again.

I weep with happy possession, I weep with submission. I weep in the grip of freedom. I am captured, I am shackled. I am not a shadow, I am a feast. I weep for more, to feel it before it is felt. My tears are warm and wet and alive, they are meant to be between her toes, they are meant to be among her fingers and upon her cheek. My tears chase the echoes and the colors of the charms. They run like contentment, they race faster than dreams. And Love makes sure I stand tall and straight as they fall.

This day has but two choices. It must walk away or kneel. I am thankful for it, for whatever it decides to do. But it must pass before I can wrap my arms around tonight. And yes, before she can even ask, I answer. My spread is wider than wings and wider than mouths, and the hunger and the feed from the humble man is nothing she wants to escape. Tonight must come before the bath of sleep, tonight must come before morning. This impossible lift, this impossible carry and task we perfect each day. This is immeasurable, this is indescribable, this is forever. It lives within the softest kisses between our lips, it lives between my butcher's arms and her dancer's legs. It warms itself between our hearts.

Before I could speak, I was spoken to, and that breath is still at my ear. The first time I heard your name is still at the most vulnerable and wishful side of my neck. The first time you rose from bed and I watched you walk and I prayed for strength, I feel those steps across my stomach. I feel them in my night legs and remember them in my day walk. The first time my hands worked to lose themselves between your hair and your back. I am still here, I am still found, I am still saved. My doubt was craving the orchard before you told me, before the river took me, before I begged to be washed out to sea. Not even you know how far I have been pushed, how deep I have been touched. Some things have occurred and been written beyond the confidence of history.

Now I scream for our nights to begin before I explode. If I could somehow be the writer and not the narrator, I could find or free a simple line or phrase from within the delicate, from the folds and the tastes and the pastries, from the crawl of the forever things. I could tell the world the secrets without ever telling them our names. I could tell them secrets, but not the secrets behind our smiles.

I will never grant light to the times before the forever things. Before I walked through the soup just to reach home. When I was a skinny narrator with the fattened push of a writer. He and I, we eat meat from the same bones and menu, and we love the same woman, and we happily plead for more.

I know your love is devastating and I can not live without it out. Before we pass these last hours just to reach those we need, before we will the minutes to take their long walk away. Before the dishes are finished and kept in all their places, before you wait in our room beneath the light and your book. Before I have had one last hard hot soak and remember there are no wounds to heal. Before I turn into melt and puddle.

I need you to feel this walk and this new discovery, this song, this promise, this elation, this bliss. I feel it soaking from your waiting legs and your moving legs, and your unmoving arm, and the whisper behind the door. I know this language. I speak a slow that is new and forever. I kiss you like you understand you spoke the words first. Before, the narrator wore his shirt, and now the writer takes him by his collar and buttons, and in a low growl says we never have to apologize for loving for so long or for so deeply. Not even when we were twisting before we were reunited.

'I just love you, Leo,' she says, and kicks her feet for me to notice. She must know I am inches before the repair, I am the man before the ruin. Her question is warm and it is in the room and taking off its own clothes. I spotted her and chased her through centuries before it was wrong or right. I am coming to bed, long after the chase is over, I am coming to bed and chasing again. The doors are hung and the locks are quiet, and I can hear Love humming in the room she threw opened to share.

The radio sits in its place, my mind is left outside to cool, the dishes are in the sink and the cabinets, the weather is beyond the walls and the only rain and wind is coming from inside. My steps are the only ones in the house, they are on a tidy path and my only attention and intentions lead me towards Love's arms. I am the only man alive who hears them and knows them. They call through the darkness, I slick my hair with the thought of them. I am being guided, and it is not just a window I have thrown opened.

And in the absolute, in the happiness, in the lingering smoke of anticipation, before the sweetness and the certainty, before the slow dragging heavenly grasp. Before I can escape what I can not see coming. The words spill across my mouth and I do not hear them. There is a darkness barking, a darkness pressing and building.

I make coffee for the morning, I make coffee for just us two. I leave a note for the morning, I leave it for only Love to see. There is the sense of a dark playing games. It is coming with legs, before I can escape, before I can be rescued. The Stranger slides his tongue across the window. He sees everything, he simply intrudes and indulges. He takes nothing. I see nothing more, but a drift has been unlocked, its appearance as sudden as a loss.

AFTER

To not have this swollen quiet morning would have been a tragedy, after surviving our night. My head is filled with every promise we did not speak. I have hands that never belonged to me and were always meant for her. I have a walk too strong for legs and too true for chairs. The only noise comes from the clouds that seem to have been drawn and dragged across the sky. I am full and I am weak, I am soft and I am lured, I am wild and remembering the taste. There is night and there is an endless night. There is night and there is night soft with skinspeak, a night longer with more words than mouths.

This morning is spraying promises the stars can not keep. This morning is a fed hunger, a thrill in a burned pan, a scorched kiss. This morning comes, hand to hand, like a spoon to the lips, a taste of the needed and had.

I am standing in the sun, realizing I have all I ever wanted. I am beyond the reach of the fortunate ones. I am already in the trap. Love has gone to work early today, and I am thankful, for this is something I do not wish for her to see. This is nothing I wish to see myself.

I squint, watching the Stranger's approach, the sun is at his back, and he is pretending to be hesitant. He vanished quicker than a thought last night, he vanished too quickly to be a memory. He has an unsettling, rattling walk. There chains which first seem

29

to follow him, I see now the roll out behind him, they lay long and unmoving. As though he senses it, or hears words I do not speak, the Stranger's face twists nearly into a smile. Charms appear from his other pockets, he brushes the insects from them, and the balance feels forced, it feels manipulated.

There is a calling to his gait, there is something I do not dare name or trust. I feel obligated to remain, obligated to stand between the Stranger and our opened door. I am suddenly the last in line, the first face in line. He is unfamiliar, he is unlike how he was on the other side of the window. He approaches in a slow loop. I stand between him and what Love and I will forever be.

He tests what will be the first lie, a probing exploratory lie. His eyes wait for the splash, wait for the ripple. 'Will you not invite a Stranger to come in out of the cold?' he says. Those words are still in my skin. It is neither cold or time for a visit. His eyes search and wrestle my silence. There were things I was to do today, things I can not remember at the moment. He wears a hat. And then he does not. The yard is filled with his fingers. He as a beard and now I see the spittle on his clean chin. He is taller than me, by a full head, and he smiles, and he is not.

There was a roast I was to put in the oven today, there is trash I was to take to the bins. Yes, she probably gets tired on days like these, at the end of long days like these. She looks tired to me. It takes an uncomfortable moment to realize someone is speaking, either the Stranger or I. 'Who?' I say.

'Love.' I have an instant of real rage and sinking sadness, hearing this strange voice speak her name. The Stranger speaks her name. He is again several paces from me, out toward the middle of the yard, out in the fall shadows that find our yard. He shows no hint of retreat, he is out of place, there, or we are out of place, there. The Stranger wears a face that knows, his hands rub a face I do not trust.

I go inside and return quickly with a push at my back. I have another coffee and a mistake and a suspicion. He is closer now, with steps that pretend they are not intruding. He is closer now and my stomach feels empty. He kicks a charm as though he is kicking a dog. He looks at me with judgement in his stare. I have no fondness for rudeness, I haven't the nature for it. I haven't the meat or the gifts for confrontation. It hasn't had a place in my life for some time. The Stranger stands as though he is comfortable, and so must I. Just as his tongue dragged across the glass, his eyes drag across the minutes. He was slightly disheveled and almost cruel, and I notice he is rather well dressed now, though more eccentrically than elaborately.

The Stranger's polished shoes are holding his stance closer. He looks at me as though he is trying to remember my name, trying to place my face to a name. And now he says, 'Will you not invite a Stranger in out of the rain?'. I drink my coffee, there is not a cloud in the sky. There is laughter and no one is laughing, there is conversation and no one is speaking. There was much to be done today.

The links of the chains are pulling themselves back into his pockets and he handles each one. There is no towel or remedy for the troubles today. Maybe not all of these are for you and Love, maybe one of these are for you and Love. Maybe your faith will be the last piece you surrender. 'Did you say something?' I ask. Now there is a chill to the air, his face is turned away from me and his face is close beside mine. I can't remember the last time I had the urge to run and hide. I must close the door. There is a scream. The Stranger steps into a charm as if it were a puddle. And the

31

dreams struggle and fade a little more. We are all awake and only one is speaking.

He leaves abruptly as though I won't remember he arrived. I must ignore the thought I am holding an empty cup on an empty day. When I walk inside, I listen for steps which aren't behind me. I am fighting against the cold that is not here, I am leaning against a wind that is not blowing. The Stranger's face returns in a flurry of old photographs. I am certain we have never met. I know we have never met.

He mentioned Love, he spoke her name, I feel the trespass, I feel the stab. I sense an old boil, I return outside with old years in my fists, I return with confidence, and I am alone. But with a taste that should have never followed last night. He is gone. I can see his figure, it moves from tree to tree, it takes the pride from the branches that have already surrendered their leaves. They bend in an ache I can almost hear. They bend and I can almost hear and agree. The Stranger is gone, and he is dancing in plain sight. He moves without consequence for what he steals. My head throbs, between the left and the right, my head throbs between realities and tenses. The past muddies the present, the future is becoming wet and wetter with twisting questions.

I want to return to Love and I and the ages, Love and I and the forever things. We create and embrace all we need, and never before struggled with the wants beyond. There is childish laughter in the distance, there is a childish game being played. There is a shiver that comes after the sunlight. What is to fear after the visit, what surely never happened after the night. I have worked my cup down to an angry emptiness, and my hand can barely hold it.

Not as we held the night, just hours ago. We held it close and we held it between us and we held it at bay. In these same arms that found waking dreams, I can now find no strength. These eyes of mine that sought and found and devoured, they do nothing but deceive me now. These lover's hands I have regrown, they are sleeping with deception. I become aware I am alone, and I am slowly backing away from the pull of it. Love will be home in a few hours and I know it will take only a look and a touch.

There is no cold and no mischief today, but I am watching the Stranger as he is watching me. I am swimming with the Stranger as he is drowning me. And this conversation is all in my mind and all I can hear. He would ask what I claim to be, I have claimed nothing. He asks with jealousy of all my rejected attempts, and I have attempted nothing. The Stranger angrily asks what it is I hide, and I know I give all I have to give. He wants me to know my history has already been written. I believe in fate and faith. He tells me the future is spent dirtier than yesterday.

The greatest risk of all was in the quiet, in the longing to be found and taken. The Stranger tells me only a fool believes lovers' dreams will save them. The greatest failure of all is never to be a failure. I feel his eyes upon me, he claims magic she will never offer. His eyes will never glow like hers, not in the closeness, not in the darkness. It will be a pleasure and a delight when the world crashes down. But his eyes will never be pools of satisfaction, not like hers.

She is Love, and love is timeless, it is a beast and an idea that tracks you and hunts you and aches for you and finds you. And if you are so fortunate to have laid down as prey, love is a taste found once, and again and over again. Love is a calm and a fury, it bastes you and cooks you and turns you slow in the dark.

The Stranger is snapping away the branches he dances across and destroying the branches he became. He asks how long will she bring me her tired shoulders and how many more days can I squeeze and massage from her feet. And how much do I relieve and how much do I contribute. The easiest and most fair is never the answer. The Stranger's smile crashes over his teeth and his words slither through his breath. The answer can come only from his will and his making. From his taking. 'And where is your pen, Johnny, and what has it done?', he says. If I were to be more than the narrator. I would tell Love all I might do.

He wants to speak of the riddles the chains possess, the chains I avoid, he laughs when I believe they are not meant for me. There are riddles in their absence, riddles that call. He speaks down like a wash, he speaks down into the blood on the inside. Love and I are not new to the world, the years are flattening, the ones which wore masks have made way for the ones that dress in dreams. I will have no reach beyond his arms, they have found me and will find me again. Love is the fruit and he is the burden.

The Stranger speaks from the back of his throat, he insists we are more than loose acquaintances and he is the apocalypse of this paradise. He is bringing me to the edge of belief, somewhere before the strings of today, somewhere after the webs of the years. He is trying to make my eyes doubt, he is making my skin a discomfort. The stretch of space between where he and I stand has a tremble, the stretch of time between he and I has an echo. The Stranger tells me he has already won, all I have to do is fall, or do nothing at all.

I have to admit I believe he is real. It would be troubling otherwise. He is somewhere in my eyes, he is somewhere between today and the past, he is out there, he wants me to hear his first song, he wants to teach me my first lie. The Stranger's eyes are in the distance, his brutal mouth is in the distance, they are pulling and pressing. The chains are laying about, they are growing restless, there is noise and impatience. They are not for Love and I. No, Johnny, but you can see them, you can see where you can no longer stand. Where you can no longer walk, no longer belong. Some of the chains speak of struggle and poverty, some speak of doubt and submission, some are senseless and some sensitive. They glow and they are not for us. The chains possess the world and the world created the chains. There are loud chains of worry and loud chains of indifference, loud chains of reluctance and rolling chains of inevitable change. There are chains of fear which choke out the familiar.

'I was just a Stranger to be invited in out of the cold,' he says. And there is nothing colder than his laugh. Love has made me too much of a gentleman, I haven't the venom to silence him. I have too much courage to run, too much courage to fight. He can not reach into our embrace, he can not tolerate the hope and the promise. We are disgusting, so he awaits, in the trees, if he must, just into the darkness, if he must. For we truly have no choice. I have unconsciously joined his conversation, and I ask him to repeat what he said and I feel his next swallow. The invitation is only after he comes, the loss is after his take and his share. The memory is after the forget. The feel is after the burn.   I have been cooked in bliss and sauced and prepared to perfection and the Stranger feels no need to hide his fork and spoon and into his shirt he buries his napkin. I stand in a storm, I stand in pride. He smiles because he has already won and tasted his fingertips and he has not aged through the years after. I do not know what I refused. The Stranger smiled. The Stranger leaps. I am two shades past the man I was this morning, I am two turns from the straight and hard into the twist. I am two questions beyond the denial. I ask him to repeat what he just said. I have no memories of meeting him before today. I am in the laces, I am beneath the lashes, after the Stranger insists, he knows me.

Love will be home soon, and I do not know how I will speak of today. We know no shadows, there are no hides, no secrets. I have no explanation that is sensible in my head. This is after the beginning, after the chaos. I never invited him, inside or otherwise, and I never closed the door. The Stranger is gone and the chains have crawled until they have nearly disappeared. The light is leaving and the winds are waking. My eyes are no longer showing my ears what they hear. The world is struggling from the corners, there are only the pieces of the before and after.

I dangle as two, as I have been and as I will always be. Love has returned as a comfort and an eruption. She uses her angel's voice and her lover's hand. I do believe I have moved from this spot today. I wear her favorite smile and speak the words I hope she never forgets. It is just us and the magic, the three in the heat. We are the mine and yours, the now and forever. We are in the bend of the whispered promise. There are but two of us again, after the return kiss, where we were and where we belong. What we know and what we learn. Love and I in the moment and all we refuse to escape. The smoke from the first long slow burn, the rhythm of the first long slow words. We are together again. Just the two of us, Love and I.

Any despair or confusion can come after, now we are tangled and free in the patience of the anticipation, in all the colors of blindness. We are in the tense jaws of tenderness. We are the menu tonight, we are the meat and the cost paid to be relished and

36

savored. We drop into the float, we need no rescue, we need no heroes. I want to tell her what I know tonight and what I will have learned by morning.

After Love comes home, the world is back upon both of its legs. Now it is only the here and the there. The need does not cry, the destination will soak. I wish just once the words would fall from me, I wish I could say them twice. Once for her to hear and once for her to feel. There are words that outlast truths and lifetimes and emotions. There are words that search and linger longer than souls. Certainly, we have been found. But there are words that drift and we unconsciously elude. There are words that refuse to learn to sink or how to fly. There are words I will speak and never speak again.

There is today and after. I have my hands and my heart, the walk and the night wait just beyond the door. I have my soul and the choice, I have the hesitation and the journey. Everything in pairs, I have discovered the splinter which splits everything in twos and halves. Love and I. The longing and the feast. The narrator and the writer. The face in the window and my own. The Stranger and the forever things.

The shiver and the glory of the night has not left my bones. It aged me into a softness that won't be surrendered. I will walk with it for the rest of my life. It was a night we found ourselves so perfectly contented and still. A night that brings mornings you never hope to survive. My face fell to her shoulder and her hands held it there. We spoke with the silence that chased after the blankets, it chased the blankets down past our feet and over our heads. We fell beyond sleep and the dreams that came after. My hands were born onto her back and her hip, her hands were born onto my chest.

Our eyes rose and opened, we were kept, we were cleaned. Two of my kisses found her high at her cheeks, just below her eyes. One for the moment we met, one for the moment we knew. She changed the stance and the heavy feel from being alive to being the living. I awoke the happiest man alive, finding her hands in mine, knowing I am the only man who will ever experience it.

Love and I laid in a moment we begged to overwhelm us. We were in the space of trust and innocence and my lips spoke their first words to her. And now after the long stretch, I know there is no price or gain or search. There is no more need, no reluctance or apologies. I understand what I will be and what I must be, with no lean and no crutch and no tricks. I understand all she wants is me, as the temperatures rise and fall, as the months grow to years and the years grow past the count. I love her as though I have never lived before.

I love her as though she has explained every mystery, I love her as though there will always be but two chairs to sit. I love her as I stand, as though I have no other voice and no other place in this world.

I am outside first, and she is coming after. I wait, she is coming with her fingers and footprints, she is coming with her ease and her might, she is coming with her long soft hair and her delight. I wonder what I will call ground and soil and elegance after this day. I sense the approach of a new season, a season of long roast and belief. The days have not become relentless, they are relentless. But each is new and we claim them as ours. We will have our time beyond the hurry, we will have our time beyond the calm. We will have ourselves after this cold is gone, we will keep ourselves. Love and Leo, it is against our faces, Love and Leo, it is upon our hearts. We are in the walk.

We are in the walk before the journey, we are in the glow, we are in the gardens. I will walk into the pleasure and trap of the snare and there my legs will stay. The work for the need's pales against the voice of the haves. I know Love feels the peace. We never drift. If I could only crumble and fail as the narrator, and after find the lovespeak of the writer. There is but one line that is waiting long after it has slept. There is something I must tell Love that is beyond perfection, it is beyond the dew, it is too rich for devotion, it is too frightening for the absolute.

It is not a confession, it is a reflection, it is the promise beneath the pool. It is eating the very stones in my soul and aching to be found. It wants to surrender its freedom and be given. It will end all contentment and doom us to bliss.

All of this suddenly ceases with a crush of a stare, I stand beneath the long look and capture of a carnivore. The Stranger's mouth shows his yellow smile. He has a long slow approach that puts him at my shoulder in a breath. His hot breath. His fingers draw jagged lines between the night and the magic and the morning. They interrupt the walk. He removes the silence from shadow, the black from darkness, and the weight from truth. The Stranger stands in front of me and behind me, his eyes are gashes and open like hungry holes. He wants to have a conversation. He wants the wait to be over and the pieces to be burning at the edges. He wouldn't mind if the sticky syrup we hide runs like rivers. He wouldn't mind a small sip of my attention and time, because he can show me how he can take away its spin. He can offer salt or heaven, either one will be soaking clasps and irons. The Stranger has the keys to the locks we refuse.

LISTENING

I know one day I will forget what he said. I know one day I will forgive myself for being the narrator. I know one day Love will forgive me and herself. To continue the story is to acknowledge the memory that is a violence upon the past and the present. I know what lurks, and I have seen it, I must close the doors at least halfway, not against the wind or the cold, against the admission of a guilt that is not ours. I have to be certain all the walls have their height today.

The Stranger told me he would not mind if it was boredom or weakness or curiosity that made me agree to a conversation. He had already held the pretty and the innocent in his hands when they were nothing more than blind infants. His hands knew the cost of reward. He wanted a conversation, if I could suffer just a few minutes. He showed me his hands were empty and there was no harm I would ever be able to see. He could grip the chance of courtesy and pull my hair from the roots if I'd like, because my only chance to run would be in my memories. The Stranger told me he would start from the finish, because it would be easier than the beginning. He said, yes, he would appreciate a chair, so he might rest his legs. He crossed one over the other, it felt good kicking me into slow surrender.

There is a cloud damp about me that separates reality from what happened. The scratch comes to the surface and the holes in the story are hungry mouths. He asked if I could feel myself hanging above the delicious crack, I would drop and he would take away all the light and all the love. The Stranger's tongue slithered around what he intended and what he offered. He asked if I knew the difference between what was clean and what was right. He uncrossed and redressed his legs and told me the past and the present did not dare bark their differences to him. The past and the present could not lay in his lap. And could I feel his thumbs pressed to my forehead, could I feel his hands thundering around my chest.

I briefly notice something retreating into his coat and the smoke escaping his lips. This is just an opportunity. A conversation about a once in a lifetime offer, a once in a lifetime risk. He has dragged lesser men screaming to the ledge. I lean in a little closer, to better understand the words I am hearing. I am listening and falling in circles. The Stranger tells me he has already scraped away half of me, and the rest of the lean bones are the best for the dirty gravy. I am listening, and he is ensnaring my senses. When he says my name, he spits it out like a poison. When he mentions Love's name, his hands and feet crawl up my back.

The air has become stale, but is growing pungent. Do I hear him? The first step is easy and I am six steps in, the last step is stumbling towards me and I can not dance from its path. The devastation is wonderful. The Stranger asks if I am seeing so I might go blind. He asks for a bit of a drink, and what difference does it make if an hour has passed and more are to be suffered. He wants to know if I am still curious to understand his reach is beyond my threshold. He admits Love and I were a foul taste, we burned into his eyes, he couldn't bathe enough to be in a room by himself. He admires the life we are creating, he is fascinated by each slow inching growth towards evolution.

I believe today has found its own place to hide, and the grass is retreating down to its roots and the birds fall from the sky. He finds our delicateness, our truth, our passion is like a thousand needles across his skin. He appreciates my offer to move to a more comfortable, shaded area, and he is not at all surprised or humbled by the fact I am still listening. He is free and ageless and tireless in his pursuit of all that is pure. I don't have anything of great urgency to do today, so I can sit with him, and take every bite of the stew, spoonful after painful spoonful.

The Stranger smiles, he never has to be courteous or gracious, he can turn comfort inside out and make it forget it was warm. Stepping upon beauty, the crunch never keeps him up at night. I wonder how long it has been since he has had a peaceful sleep. He says not since he broke the will of the willful, not since he doused the light of a dream.

He has gained my empathy. I apologize for not inviting him sooner. He would be grateful if I would not speak while I listen. Promises have cream inside, and promises made between lovers have life and blood inside. He laughs because the promises are kept and clung to not as though our lives depended on it, but our souls hold them so tightly. If I answer his questions, he has a blunt tool and a carving tool, to keep me from protesting as he leads me down the wrong path.

I will never know, I will never hear the tearing, the collapse, the surrender of soulmates. The Stranger says he will pull my words out of my thoughts. I can only see light. I see the hope of light. I see the depth. He vomits on the lawn and walks through it. Because he thinks we are perfect for submission. Our faith is something he can not abide. It is such a rare gruesome infection in this world. Our song is a place for his boots. Love and I and the forever things bring his jaws to a grind. It is so full, he must create a hole. I think it strange, he and I have never met before.

I will sit and listen for as long as he wishes to speak. I will never admire his charismatic claws, I will never drown in his swim. The thought of Love makes me want to stand, he demands I sit, and he pulls away the rope. My Love is gentle and giving and the Stranger chokes on something at the back of his throat. I refill his glass and listen a little longer. He is waiting until it becomes too dark and too cold and too late for me. I listen through the menace and I listen through the thorns. I haven't the grit I had hours ago. I inch towards the blindness, he will teach me to run. His eyes have discovered the weakness, and it is taking a wash in his stomach. It wasn't Love and I. It was me. Love and I gripped so tight, and he found my hands to work upon.

The Stranger tells me he has been eavesdropping through the walls, he has been spying through the windows, he has been counting our steps, he has been counting our kisses. He has been watching and he is repulsed. He has heard every word and read every note and he is sickened beyond relief. He doesn't marvel at my consistency, he thinks nothing of my devotion, he wants to set fire to it. I smile and thank him. Love is my muse, she is the pursuit I hold and no longer chase. She is my heart and my soul. The Stranger unleashes a grinding wrenching belch. He would smash my hope if he hadn't already had it by its throat.

It is getting darker and I am waiting for the Stranger to break his silence. Love will come home soon and her possession will lose his fascinating grip. My legs will be loosed from the concrete and my short hairs will uncurl and his hands will release my face and I will be breathing again. His smile that cast me vulnerable will become snake again and unseen again. The Stranger pretends to plead with me.

'I want to make you famous,' he says.

He says it and shovels the ashes from a wish I never made. He is leaving before the light returns. I am feeling a bit empty and exhausted. He says something into the trees about being famous, suffering famously. I shiver, it is suddenly freezing. My mind hums blankly, and a whole day has been lost. I nearly panic, and grab a broom and try to sweep away the shadows. I feel I have been in a battle. I feel as though I know the grinder.

I need a soft dream tonight, I give Love a kiss when she comes home, I kiss both her tired shoulders. She wonders where I have been. She knows, she knows. I try to trace the ache down her arms, I try to chase it away. We will have an easier life. We agree the setbacks and struggles are temporary. We are in agreement, about the glue and the hold of the riches. We are in search of a different reward.

Fatigue is a distraction from the Stranger tonight, it is a distraction from everything that isn't candy tonight. And silence is its soup, as we lay together in our thoughts. Nothing is wrong and tomorrow is fixed. It lays about in repairs, waiting. I rise and go outside one more time, out into the night. One paralyzing step into the night. I am disappointed to see them, some hiding and some daring the light. The chains are waiting and pretending to sleep. Chains for the hollow, chains for the loud, chains for the worried. Chains for the empty hands and the monthly bills, chains for the slowdowns and the stoppages, for the lack of understanding. Chains for trying and for the heavy heavy minds. They try to laugh at today and the way we hold hands and say it without words. They try to laugh at tomorrow and the hope it brings.

The chains can't belong here, we work too hard, and we don't ask with our two mouths or two fists. They don't belong here are we don't hide. Our backs work as though they were younger, and we pretend we will have them when we are older. There are chains with eyes and chains with ears and chains with open grasping reaching links. I will lock them out of our home, I will lock them out of our room. The chains that cling and crawl and call. I will keep them from our bed. I shouldn't speak of today and the Stranger, there should never be another day like it. All the while, Love awaits with what I wish to never escape. I succumb like a lover, I search like a soul, she speaks in a voice of trust I will never fail. Behind our door is welcome and comfort, starlight and lace. Behind our door is a hushed world and a slowed time and lightning that drops like whispers. The weather is released within the ease of lovers finding their hands. These are the spoils that spill across stomachs, these are the trophies made from chests, this is the devotion escaping through the skin of arms and legs. These are the true muscles of Time, they press the door closed and press upon the walls, they lift us and plead with us. Understanding grows wet and turns to steam, acceptance is long hoarse and rests its gentle voice. The warmth feels like sand and the chills feel like syrup. We forget everything we need. And we learn only what we want. Nothing is unseen and nothing is unheard and nothing asks for forgiveness. Love has placed me in careful playful piles again.

A minute in this light can steal a century from the dark. There is a breathless shared fury before the pause, the pause that bows to the hold. The hold that brings the end to the night and seduces us in the gentle hours and makes the dawn slow and sleep with us. All that is beautiful begins again. All that is beautiful rises first.

And all that is frightening must find itself, all that is burdensome must find itself. All that lingers must find its own way. All that doubts must find its own pieces. As we lay buried, happily buried, with my hand in your hair and your arm through my chest, my knee on your hip and your feet at my calf, your eye in my ear and my good morning at your mouth. As we are buried in all the forever things.

I am too late for the night and the morning comes like spiders and silk. The Stranger is bringing his steps, he is approaching and retreating, sidestepping and stomping. He wonders if it is too early to ask if I have considered all he has said. It is indeed too early to remember anything he said. I can still hear Love's last kiss. His speech is a bit too aggressive and he comes with a shadow that he tilts aside with a long hat and a shifted grin.

The Stranger uses the callouses in his throat when he says he is disappointed I have not surrendered my senses. He is dismayed we have wasted this much time, his voice rises as high as a violin and comes like a dagger. He has not yet been fully invited and he suspects I will not ask him to leave. I haven't the courage or the coarseness to force him to leave. I have asked him for nothing and that matters even less. With my abundance of caution, I have once again failed to close the door. When the door is left open the Stranger uses his legs, and when there is a break in the conversation, he uses his hands.

I feel his words striking me, his gifts are bold and his gifts are selfish. If I agree to sit with him, he will allow me to ask questions and he will answer the correct ones. As a courtesy. Like a hanging fog. Because I nod and acknowledge, I feel hopeless, I am falling. Acknowledgement is the first step towards losing. I won't dare wipe at my eyes with his handkerchief, he puts it away, for now, it growls in his pocket.

My mind struggles with his manner of speaking. It is disgusting and punishing and penetrating, his tongue contradicts one side of his mouth and then the other. It is slowly becoming irresistible. It is a trance that isn't love, it is a dare that stinks of failure. He offers to answer the questions I have not yet asked. Because he is timeless, he is experienced, he can envision the end before the beginning. He is the serpent, and I will give him permission to bite painfully.

The Stranger's name is unfit for my lips and it burns my throat. He passes me a card, and I recognize the letters written, in a hand and a pen I have never seen. He never said he would make me famous, he said he will bring me to fame. He does not simply change lives, he takes them and returns them unrecognizable. He rolls words backwards and inside out to cover and release the ones he just spoke. He is not going to change our pitiful lives, he despises them, he is going to expand them. He insists I stop speaking of serenity and beauty, he has yet to show me his version.

The Stranger already has it in his grip, he can pull at any moment. But there is no satisfaction, no reward, it is meaningless and painless if I am not first fully aware. I must be conscious of the thread, of the shred within me, he seeks to exploit. He is not the hammer, I am the weakness. I will understand why he speaks of me in the past tense. He refers to me as a memory, not one he will keep, but others, he supposes, others may.

I never asked for fame. I never asked for more than what we have. He asks which of the hills Love and I choose to climb will lead us anywhere. These hills have one side and we will return to the beginning, time and again. Just another tired beginning. It will be ours, yes, and we will call it ours, it will be precious. And he would like to set it on fire.

I will never comprehend his resources. His laugh is long and horrific. He has openly stolen from the world at will, he has done it for so long he has outlived objection. His existence is oily persuasion, it is the weakness and willing blindness of others. He will sing a melody of trust, and everyone will sing along. Only he understands fully, everyone needs help to climb from the cold, everyone needs help to walk out of their sleep. He will remove the difficulty even if it means introducing the panic and the fear. He will take his share, he will be paid his price. I don't know what he wants, but I will speak with Love today, we will talk about it today.

I don't know what he wants. The Stranger wants to jump upon me, he wants to use his poison and spear. He wants the long slow walk into me and the longer walk away. He wants to laugh at what my eyes know. He wants to taste my faith on toast and hear me cry in the night. He will make me famous. For his price.

The Stranger assures me, we will learn to live with the guilt of having what we never had. He invites Love to come to the very edge and not one more step. Because he knows I have already crossed and I am alone. Perhaps one day I will again see that blue in her eyes. I do hear what he is saying, and I have heard everything he has said. The Stranger never pays an apology, he has never felt remorse. He has never spoken a word untwisted, he has never said anything he can't reverse. He will offer what the world can not offer. For me, it is the slide, for me it is the slow leak. He never once uses his mouth to frame this as the one chance to make our wildest dreams come true. He never offers any reward he can not take from me.

He has no weapons in his hands, and he barely uses them as leverage. He pokes and prods at the pieces he creates. I am willing to do nothing, and I am surrendering nothing. And yet he can hear me screaming down the well. He finds it all delicious but no where near his price. I don't understand how he speaks to me, he is describing my soft undersides, he is describing the path I should not have taken. He speaks as though I am there and here and never before and never again. He is feeding it to me by the spoonful, the mouthful, and he is telling me I am choking. The Stranger is speaking with six voices and he is not speaking at all. This is the slide I haven't the patience for, the slide which eludes my own faith and frustration. It has been mine from the beginning. It has been mine and mine alone. It is already too late to change my mind. He has listened to our every word and has watched our every movement. He has heard every secret we have kept, he has read every note I have written. He knows of the book I wrote just for Love, he knows of Cupid and he knows of the Muses. We are a terrible and a tenderness he can not abide. And if I am insistent, if I pretend to be honorable and courageous, he knows exactly what it is, what I will sacrifice. Because it is already too late and I have come too far. I have allowed too much.

I have not once stepped beyond the comfort and the familiar. I have not once gone past this holding dream. I can not speak his name, and he calls me Johnny once more. Johnny, to make it dig deep, Johnny, to make it burn. The Stranger smiles and tells me Love and I should begin to regret and wish we had never spoken our dreams aloud. He was not searching for us, and that was the first price he collected. He would never possess us, and that was the second price we paid. He was unnoticed for as long as he needed to be, but he was never careful, he is never careful. We couldn't see and we couldn't hear, someone is to blame. I couldn't see, I couldn't hear, the fault is mine.

The Stranger speaks and whistles me into a cage. It is rather unimportant that I am listening. Love and I are but a diversion, an amusement. We are a feather, a trinket, a pause in always. He never denies himself the taste of temptation. His intended destination and deception can wait, it will wait. You can not escape what you do not know is coming. We are going to pay someone else's price, and in the future, soon, someone will pay ours. He speaks as though all of this has happened. 'You are no longer bending, Johnny, I have twisted you,' he says. The past can not be unlived and unfelt.

To slide from narrator to writer, it is not part of the game, it is not a challenge. He tells me he doesn't even have to pull his boots on for this performance, but he will, and he'll use them. I write for her and only her, sometimes it is clever and even honest. There would have been no harm, leaving things as they were. There would have been no harm if he had taken a glimpse and simply passed us by. He smelled Love and I before we caught his eye, and I was the easier target. He speaks to me like scissors, like rivers burning. He could have finished with me in just one night. But he sensed all I could lose.

I don't remember asking for anything, and it is though I can't refuse the offer of the shame and discomfort of fame. I am already within the brutality of the slide, what I feel is irrelevant. The Stranger tells me everyone has a dream that places them in that dark corner. Fear has only one face and he has hidden it from me already. He doesn't even have to wear his gloves for me, but he will. Some have asked to be queen and were granted castles, and there was time to endure before the walls crumbled. Some wished for adventures and there were successes to endure before the failure. I have already ripened into the fall.

I ask him if we might move into the sunlight, I am feeling a sudden chill. He assures me we can be anywhere, anywhere at all, because now is gone and it is too late. I am mud and mud I will remain. He tells me I will never be grateful and I will never forgive him.

The Stranger spins his tale of his perfection and his purpose in this world. He won't bore me with the names and the faces I will not remember. The day is always of his choosing and the chaos is always his creation. He asks is it even bearable to sit with him, and no, no it is not. He speaks of me with disgust and destruction, he speaks with his tongues wrapping around my head. I attempt to stand against this twisting sensation, and he corrects the slide, and redirects the slide. I am listening to what he has done. He tells me to picture the beauty of Love's face because it walks across all that I see. It is the first thing he will take, it is the last thing I would offer.

The transformation I could not manage, he needed only to brush the words hanging from my lips. He took me beyond doubt and return. There is another moment of madness within the manner the Stranger speaks. It is as clear as anything I know. We had to see it to completion, all of us, we had to prolong it and suffer it and enjoy it until the very end. All of us. All that awaits has transpired behind us. I must need more of the knuckles beneath his gloves, more of the stamp beneath his boot. This day is his, he has possessed it.

'Those hands of yours, Johnny, I threw them away. That face of yours, I don't remember it,' he says. The groan and the ache of listening to him talk, I find myself unable to rise from my chair. He tells me some needed brilliant lights and some needed blinding noise, some needed sickness and some needed recovery. The endless list is longer than the arm he effortlessly throws across the lawn. Mine will be easier, he will hardly need to wake anyone. It was planned in a moment and carried out with an inaudible cry.

The Stranger is so certain of what has happened and what is to come. He tells me I can stand if I must but I can not walk from this offer, this slow crawling movement, this slow painful expansion. He has already told me it is like the wretched evolution we speak of so often. I no longer understand the ridiculous and the unreasonable. His hands have five fingers and now they have six. His hands have seven fingers and now they have mine. He will give me an evening to pretend I am hers.

We are going to board a train, out of this sleepy village, out of my sleepy reluctance. His train, yes, he has means I can not imagine, he creates dreams I can not imagine. I am in his second longest grip and beyond understanding. Fame is not what I asked for and wished for, it is the price he demands. He laughs at the impossibility of it. Five days upon a train is the cost and the consequence. Five is the round number he chose. It is for the words that dangle, for those I want Love to hear. It is a chance for the storm I can't live without. It is the one thing he discovered I can not resist. There will never be another way. Five insignificant days of his choosing, five insignificant days at his pleasure. I will never find another way. He is chewing at the side of my head.

The sunlight grows too warm and I drag into the shade. The Stranger tells me he has never kept a promise, and he promises me he will abandon me and not remember me. Only Love must know. He'll allow us an evening, she can hold me in the winds that blow against us. She can smile and think of waking to days of ease I could never provide. He will allow me to keep my promises, because he has no need for them. I will speak with her, because I am already his. I will speak with her, because he has no need for me.

He insists I speak with Love, and tell her all we have that can not be touched, all our riches can not be taken. They can only be surrendered and he laughs at what I will sacrifice for her to hear that I have already nearly spoken. I feel it about my jaw and my waist, I feel it in my heart. Is there more hunger once you have had the experience of a lifetime. He is going to leave enough space for a long wonderful night. Once he is gone, I know this is nothing he has given or offered. This is what he can not possess.

A night on this earth, a night in this life, with our feet upon the same ground. Love is an angel the devil can not imagine, Love is a force that does not ask or take. Love is a surrender, Love is a state. There is no worship or reverence, just a hand placed at my face, where it is needed most.

I may have an opportunity we would have never found, I may be drowning in what we can not endure. To risk nothing is to risk it all. And Love sits with patience, listening as I recount everything I do not understand. There is a chance I can not take without her. Or we can be as we are, in bliss, in harmony, untouched. We can hold what we know and never escape. I ask for her voice to tell me what to do.

Love wonders how he came upon me and filled me with dread, and how he came upon us. He knows of my two books and watches through the windows and listens through our walls. This should all be wrong and he screams of it. I don't know if he speaks the truth, I believe he speaks his truths. Love says there is nothing to risk, we will always be us, we will always have us. To gain nothing is to lose nothing. Five days is so brief and sounds so long.

I wonder what it can possibly change. Love assures me again there will be no harm.

Three days ago, I would have known I was strong enough. I can not explain what has changed. The Stranger is so confident and insistent and mocking. Love asks when I would leave. I do not know, I know only it will be on a train. It somehow must be by train. For all we have, it would do no harm to perhaps have the everyday things become a little easier. The strangeness of it stiffens the room, the curtains hang like ice, the floor growls. We will decide in the morning. Love places her head on my shoulder first. And then I place my head upon hers. She stretches her fingers through mine. There is something so pure and right in this moment. We are in a place the Stranger can not take.

We lay in a moment that should not be moved, we lay in a promise that should not be touched. Each of us silently know there are dreams that belong and dreams that don't. She pulls the cover over my arm against the cold that feels like a stare. We breathe the lightness of forever, here in the dark that lays before the words I seek. I wait for the want that brings me to count my hands and touches and kisses like sheep. I wait for the breath that pulls us closer without the Stranger at our backs.

Nothing has changed except for that which we can not see. My Love and I, we are in a loveruin for two, a lovedelight for two. And I am praying into forever, I am the only one who hears his voice, asking if there isn't something more we could never need or want. The Stranger's shadow waits for an answer it has already heard and he tries to put his teeth between our long sleeping embrace.

This must be a new fire I feel at her breast, it comes through a sigh from behind her hair. For a moment I believe I can wake and walk tomorrow as I have and as I was. For a moment it is Love's familiar at my ear, Love's truth at my ear.

SLIDING

A day has passed, and a second and stretches and threatens the same. I find myself outside for many of the hours, and so does Love. We have eaten meals in near silence, taking turns looking out the windows. We are busy at our usual paces, we are restless. We are waiting. It is unusual, it is unsatisfying. A third day is approaching, it is growing inevitable. A tension is growing, it is breathing inside, it awaits outside and paces, it covers real steps, it searches like a hunter and retreats like a victim.

Something was offered, or seemingly offered, something we had never asked for. There is a subtle lack of conversation between us, it isn't uneasy, but it is aching to be noticed. Love has yet to have the gasp of meeting the Stranger. She wonders if perhaps he is a snakecharmer, perhaps he is a wanderer, a medicine man of sorts. If I can keep her from him, I will. I have the Stranger's card in my pocket, I feel my thumb running across it. I have absently looked at it, I have secretly looked at it. There is only an unfit name and nothing else.

There is what hangs beyond and heavily now. A chance we never considered. An opportunity we never needed. A question we never asked. Perhaps things will change for the better. I want to tell Love, there is no man alive who wants more for her. She knows, it is at the edges of her eyes. There is nothing more she needs. The day's work and worth, and that of tomorrow, they are nothing we can not manage.

We can escape and show each other tonight, working hands are not simply savage hands. They offer the most intimate

55

affections, they speak, they endure, they, too, thirst for gratification. They are the first to volunteer and the last to submit. They carry dreams, the ones they own. They don't disappoint, but occasionally, in the quiet, they have earned their right to feel disappointed. In the dropping darkness, ours is all we can see.

Neither of us will be the first to cast a sigh, neither will be the first to admit. I have dreamed of better things for her. I slide a little further into my chair and our silence, I slide into deeper understanding. I have been forgotten. I will never love another. She throws a sleepy eye towards me. And yesterday, today, and tomorrow fall aside. She smiles and says, 'Thank you for your note this morning.' She asks for nothing more.

The Stranger is coming with his digging boots and the ground is crawling to be free from him. He comes with a bitterness that twists our mouths and causes our hands to break from each other. He is coming with a purpose and an anger, the night is falling before him, he stoops and uses his knees to painfully cross it. He walks as one who comes to take. The chains are flowing around him and behind him. The sky is bleeding purple and the violence in his eyes is stunning, the disgust in his eyes runs out like dogs before him.

'Enchanted to meet you, the pleasure is mine,' he says, taking Love's hand. There is a brief icy moment. There is nowhere to hide, there is nowhere to hope. He has already been invited, he sits heavily onto a chair and tells Love he knows why she is my muse. She is absolutely ravishing and he will not allow her to hear him say it twice. She could have been the reason history was not written and the gods would never harm us with art. I see his face is horribly altered and he looks nearly human now and his voice is not the same. Love seems to shelter within her own arms and

56

legs and I feel the drums playing in my chest. He is refined and charming and we can barely hear him when he tells her I am the most rare and delectable meat. He would love to hear our story but he can't tolerate when we speak.

The Stranger has come with his nails and grip, he has brought the eyes that found us. He has changed his clothes and brought his laughter. He will have us, one above and one in the fire. He will possess us. If I am the choice, I would have Love hear not another word. But he has nothing to prove and nothing to justify, so he will speak and we will listen.

'But why Leo, and how did you find him?' Love says. He bristles at the question and bites into the clouds as they roll closer. He will explain soon enough and soon enough will tolerate no more questions. Consider it philanthropy, and his own amusement. The names of those who suffered his attention is a list longer than our wretched affection. The names of those who could not endure is a list longer and more wretched than our kisses.

'Why Johnny?' he says. He changes my name as though he is changing a face. Because everyone, every single one, has forgotten their birth and their name, they have forgotten their place. The Stranger chooses his price and claims his price. He says neither of us may again agree to look into a mirror. I can feel Love and I trying to twist together. His words are thick and clear and they burn rolling from his tongue. He would take a glass of wine if we would offer one. He would enjoy most anything as we continue this treacherous slide, this wreck, this havoc we have invited. We were blind and deaf to his approach and he forgives us for not anticipating his arrival, and for still not anticipating his slow hungry meal. He is who and what and where he has always been. And the world alive, and the world dead, can do nothing about it.

Love is inside, finding glasses and wine. I feel his hand at the back of my neck. He is nowhere within reach. An old wind blows and here it clings, it brings hooves to my smile. The cost won't be everything I have and everything I know, but I will wish it so. The Stranger won't leave my arms and legs so I can search through my bewilderment, search out my pride. Love returns with glasses and wine we do not drink. He accepts because we are pale before his wisdom and culture and experiences. He has drank with kings and watched them pass. He has drank with lords and then fed them to lions.

I want Love to be free of this slide. She comments on his unusual accent. And he questions if he has chosen the right one. It is my responsibility, my chivalry, that shields her. The Stranger is guessing my weight in gallons. He is guessing my weight in sleepless nights and guessing my height in torn mornings. 'So why Leo?' she says. He laughs and we nearly spill our glasses. I am an accident, I am a sideshow, I am a weed who forgot it wasn't supposed to flower. I leap from my chair, when he says what he will make of me. I want the deep intrusive chill of the Stranger to leave. I want what we had only days ago. He is rubbing his hands to make fire with no warmth. He is licking his lips to prepare words we should never hear.

'Why Johnny?' he says again. He asks us to imagine walking through a forest and finding a perfect tree. It can't be allowed to grow, it can't be allowed to hide. It must be sliced and chopped and gnawed into pieces, its bark must be pulled like hair from a head. I look from his face to Love's, to see if she is hearing the same words I hear. Inventors do not think, painters do not see, singers make no sounds, lovers make no fabulous ruins, and writers eat their fingers. The Stranger has the absolute appetite for the absolute worst. He has a howl no night can disguise, he has a greed no charity can conceal. He speaks in the awful tongues he has learned, and he has always walked free.

It is not exhaustion or the hour growing later, it is the fatigue he brings, the way he handles time and space by their legs. He sits directly between us, he is starving for neither of us, but seems to forbid anything he does not say. He croaks and then lunges at the silence and is amused as it runs away. He is trying to explain in the simplest of words.

The Stranger offers five days, which will not bring the fame I never asked for. Five days is what I must surrender to, five days is what Love and I must tolerate. The rest he will take, the rest he will conquer. The rest we will forfeit. It may be the promise of the unknown and the unneeded, it may be a breath into the truth, it may begin a stagger into the wise. He could squash every insect he sees tonight, whether they deserve it or not. He assures us, the hours will build painfully into days, the days will pile and he will be certain they pile high, they will test us and free us and destroy us. And he will break every promise he makes. He will not pretend to protect us or respect us and we will not defy him. He stands between Love's reaching hand and my own. We could agree to be a bargaining piece, one that makes him agree to stop the hunt, to pause for seasons, to remove his tongue.

The Stranger suddenly stands and pretends to look upon a watch and act as though he is late and that he may ever tire. He shakes my hand vigorously, I am a banquet that will ride his train. And he thanks Love so dishonestly for being the one to grant permission, to lose everything like a cobweb falling from a sleeve.

He says this may only be a new chapter of an old book. This may not even be a shiver into a slide. This may be a tale he has told other lost children and we may not be lost at all. But as he stands here, he promises, we won't remember the last turn. Love asks when I am supposed to board the train.

I watch as he lurks and he wants to be so close, and there is something about her that keeps him at bay. He prickles and bristles and can not bear to touch her in any way. I feel a blow to my insides. 'In two days, as I have said,' the Stranger repeats the seven words he has never uttered. He lingers while leaving, he pauses just enough to keep me in dismay.

There will never come a day Love and I remember all the splintered pieces he said. We will never remember the exact day the slide brought us into his mouth. The Stranger walked away for not the final time. I felt for a handful of Love's hair and I never needed a kiss as much as I needed now. Or then. Our wild eyes were so unclear. These legs that are here and telling this story were taught again. Arms that knew and knew such a forever were like shadows. I can try and try to step away from what happened to us. The night had a fever, I remember it all.

Love's blue eyes clear again, the Stranger is gone and he will never have us. His speak is no longer holding us. Is this trust or something that falls from above. I can't speak with anger and I can't speak with curiosity. I can barely move the breath from my chest. Love finds me like a blanket, and in a quiet moment tells me where we belong. It is she and I, at the feet of forever, it is she and I, in the hands of forever. The forever things walk with steps that are sultry and luscious, they stir the movements that can not be touched. Love is a feel, and she lets down her hair. Love is a beast.

As I allow the slide to fall from my shoulders, the magic came from a whisper, the whisper becomes a taste, the taste is a lifetime, the lifetime is an experience. Love lets me know she is alive, and the ache follows, and we are simply a woman and a man, staring into the eyes of what we know. We are a woman and a man in the most basic of our need and being. It is nearly nine and there is not a heat we can not stand within, there is not a want we did not create, there is not a will we are not called to, back to chest, in the draining dark, in the maddening unraveling, in the oil of the truth. In the forgiveness of the slide, standing in the mirror, one against one.

The forever things have stumbled upon us. As though they need to preach against the preacher. They can strike their rain upon my face. I am cleansed, I am had. The forever things come to hunt against the hunter, even though he won't be broken.

Neither of us understand the fragmented conversation, the style and the will and the speech of the Stranger. Perhaps it is best not to revisit, it is best we didn't hear what we know was said. Five days upon a train, I have never heard of such a thing. We can define it as a beginning, most beginnings are brief. We will concentrate on the next two days without anticipating the excruciating separation. I can convince myself it is temporary, it has no light or weight in forever. I am not troubled, it is some other man who is troubled.

The hours come with earnest, as though proving how quickly time may pass. I will never know the dread of absence, I will never feel its shock. There is a faint laughter in the distance and I name it the wind through the trees. I am persuading myself, this can be done. The first step will be the easiest. I am remembering the ramblings of the Stranger. The second step will finish you. I should abandon what I believe I know and embrace the simplicity. I should realize I am deaf and blind.

The Stranger nearly hissed the words. Did she marry a coward. That I can't prepare myself to unlearn what I wasn't taught. To let go of what I hold. I hear Love's tremble, and her whisper. We risk nothing and we will lose nothing. We are never apart, we are never in the past. She wears me like a jacket, and I wear her like an enchantment. The ghosts are gone, she says, the ghosts are gone, my love, let him call you Johnny for five days, you are my Leo, you will come home. We have the truths of forever, the truths for every hand, we have more than we can hold.

Love and I stand at a mesmerizing fire, we warm like clay pots. I'll call this the night before. Because I can't call it the last. My mind has surrendered all thoughts of tomorrow and the smoke has taken their place, the flames occupy their space. The fire is in a slow slide of a burn. We have nothing to forget and everything to remember. We will be fine, we will perfect. This fire feels almost like five days, and then the wood helplessly crumbles and collapses before our eyes. I find her in the dark, she knows me, I am her favorite.

I may have been uncertain an hour ago. The train is not change, it is evolution, it is unexpected surprising evolution. The kind that can run like a dog or lay like a mystery. Love found the meandering route along the map, the parts she remembers the Stranger speaking of, all of the unusual and unheard of places. She says it seems to be a purposeless path drawn by a hurtful, purposeful man. We both pause and wander and forget, I will try to look at it later. For now, my head doesn't seem to be in its proper tilt, it doesn't seem to be my own. It was slightly so, and now it is rudely so, since I drank wine with the Stranger. I drank wine from the Stranger. I can almost hear his voice, the stumble will not navigate the slide.

If I could tell her how beautiful she is tonight, we could live as though tomorrow will never happen. Tomorrow I will travel with the destination of five days. I will arrive with empty hands and no possessions, not so much as a razor or a sense of will. Those were his specific instructions. He was precise with his language, my back still aches from it, and Love, she says only that the smoke is getting into her eyes. The uncomfortable unknown and the pepper in his talk. The Stranger said he was not only a menace but tailor, not only a terror but a manipulator, and he enjoys only the finest things in life. He wants me to arrive as a clean broken slate. The side of my head feels flattened by his last words. The memory of them seem to come from the fire.

Be certain to arrive on time and sick and weak, the Stranger said. 'I have pills for that, Johnny, I have blame and shame for that,' he said. And we are to keep our goodbyes brief and tasteless before he rips our hands apart. I will slide into the fall and the fall will be cold, and it will be mine. He told Love to take shelter in what we shared because the rest belongs to him.

If I could tell Love of the feel of this night, it feels of a night we have never known. It was born from the madness of reason and given no name. We speak only our own, into the fire, into the slide. I am upon my back, in the grass, into the grass. I write her name in the sky above. I write it as it sounds, as it possesses. I will somehow recover from this wish to be the writer and not the narrator. I will recover from this fall, knowing this is not the weakness the Stranger desired, this is pleasingly important to me. If Love will promise to never call me by another name and never know be by another face.

'No, Leo, you will always be mine,' Love says. It is as though we paused and we will feel more of his hands now. I close my eyes in ecstasy in the darkness I create, I see her face. I am not in the lightning. I am not in the river. I am not the lost. I am the willing possession. Love can never be faint, she can never be timid, I feel her even now pulling me past the shrieks. I won't have to ask her to bring me to the depths of this night, she won't have to make me believe this isn't the last. There is no end and there always will be, in the toss and churn of forever.

'You will always be mine,' I say. And I hold her as though these pages are marked and the harm is already spent and we are somewhere in the spring in our gardens. At the same time, the Stranger is lifting and erasing his distance, he is approaching us as though he is colorblind to all that he will take. And before and within this fire, there is not a light that can squeeze between our embrace or our next kiss.

UNWAKING

In this slow chanting closeness, in this blistering unwaking, I don't feel stolen, I fear I can't be found. Love is a breath and an inch from my side. The day has now come. It isn't clever enough to speak, it just waits, trying to find the courage to interfere. I am wearing my morning face, hoping to find my best face before Love's eyes open. I need her to teach me to be awake, I have somehow forgotten. I wait for the strength to leave our bed, I can't reach the cold floor. I am here, I am hers, and the rest feels incredibly small.

It is today, this is the Stranger's day, Love and I admit it without speaking a word. It is today and I will lay here for the purpose of being late. These moments belong to us and they can't be taken. These moments are ours and they have a taste I believe I will need. I am feeling possessive. This is our hour, these are our hands, this is our kiss. I lay with the focus to not hear the walls grumbling and the doors calling. My lips need one more grip upon her cheek. I wait for one more breath to heave. I need her magnificent conquering wonderous eyes. I am unwaking, and my throat is too dry for words, and now she smiles because she hears me.

This morning is growing dangerously late and impatient. I am beginning to question why I agreed to this at all. I am uncertain, even as Love prevents the panic. She kisses me once, she kisses me five times to last the days. I will never leave this burning, I will never leave this tremble. My Love is simply exquisite, she is divine today, she will own my memory. We are going to lose this day, whether by force or forgetfulness. When we walk out the door it will be forever closed to today and whatever finds us.

But I am unwaking and it is pulling at me like a sickness. I don't know why I keep asking her if she will find me and find me through and again and find me five and six times. The fabric of Love's dress feels like forever and I feel the burden of leaving. We have rediscovered our first dance and are nowhere near our last, our mouths are swollen all the way down through our legs, our hearts don't drift from the promises we have made. Before we load into the car, I want one more handful of soil and need, one more handful to carry me because I can't manage this unwaking.

Love takes the long meandering route, heading towards the only railroad tracks we know in this village. They lay unassuming and unused, they disappear into the woods and I have never heard anyone say where they lead. To travel by train seems odd, perhaps mysterious, and quaint. But it is necessary and part of the pain and part of the plan, that is what the Stranger told us. Our hands clench softly together during the ride. I ask her to drive a little slower. We are nearing the closest thing to a kiss goodbye that we have ever known. She wipes at my eyes and says, 'My sweet Leo.' In the cavernous night we agreed everything would be all right, in its silence we swore everything would be all right.

At the end of a nearly forgotten dirt lane, we come to a cluster of vehicles and a hub of activity. There are slack faced uniformed hands everywhere. Massive crates and countless boxes are being moved and loaded. It seems excessive for a five-day journey. She asks if I remembered to bring everything? I will remember us and nothing more. The train is as impressive as the Stranger claimed, it is a glimpse of his impressive endless means. It can shock like a bullet and reach like a rocket. And I will be the worst that has ever set a foot inside. I stare towards the sun, remembering he said that. We are parked and sitting for a few moments and I am feeling something similar to regret and nearly wonder aloud what would happen if we simply drove away. I can count seven cars like vertebrae of the snaking train, I can think of seven reasons not to board.

Despite the growing, gnawing unwaking, there is a taste of apology at the back of my throat. We walk towards the train, I am sorry for what I have done, I want to tell Love I am sorry, before I even understand. No one is speaking, no one looks towards us. The Stranger appears, he is visibly angry, triumphantly angry, at me, at them, at us.

He tells me I am late and I should get my last kiss from her because there will be none upon the train. There is work to be done and miles to be made and I can simply continue to fade and crumble. He whispers in an unintelligible tongue and some workers vanish and some immediately hustle. The Stranger looks at Love and his skin flashes a crawl, his mouth flashes a cruelty and then remembers a smile. 'Enchanted, of course, again and indeed, see you in five days,' he says. I do receive my kiss and it feels terribly brief, her hands drop from my face and she nods towards the train. I'll remember her breath at this moment, I will remember her courage. I have nearly forgotten how to walk. I take one final look and offer a waive, it is after all only a stretch of time too shy to be a week.

Once I have passed through the first door, I am again gripped by the unwaking. I am here and lost. There is only slow forward movement now, he is taking the past. I round a corner trying to find my way. That which was a train is now a maze. The light does not fit my eyes and the sounds listen and speak as though strained. I encounter a woman or what I assume must have been a woman, she has a horrible face and is insisting I can not go forward and I can not go back.

The Stranger appears unexpectedly and suddenly at my side. He is close like a knife and plunges like distrust. He tells me the invited have no place here. There is no time, but he will show me what I must see and where I am not welcome. He will tell me the terror of the beginning and repeat it until I beg for the end. He senses I am unwaking and he gathers it as though hovering with cupping hands above a simmering pot. There will be a quiet and cold place for me soon enough, I will be told only what I must know and I will be unraveling by nightfall.

The Stranger leads me down corridors and I am grateful when he is not speaking. There are no seats within this train, only compartments with closed doors. They seem to want to yawn open as I pass, and I am told this one I will never see and that one I will know. He finds it marvelous to speak at the beginning of an endless journey. He opens a door to a room, there is but a fine table and a finer chair and nothing more. I don't remember where we are going, the map has been rained upon, the destinations are smears. Never mind where we travel and never mind it seems we are the only ones here. He wonders if I feel the swallow of the unwaking. He removes his coat perhaps to show me his arms. He tells me to remember who I am and who I am not.

This unwaking has me questioning if the train is moving. Something made me stagger, something caused him to disappear briefly. He wants to show me this room, the one I have already seen. There is now a bed for a night and the window is gone. There is a magnificent table and a magnificent chair. And his tools hang upon the walls and his tools rest in unpacked boxes. I am a withering flame and he is the heat. There is paper and pen and a lamp and he will do the rest. The Stranger reminds me the moment is coming and I was willing and now unwaking.

I don't understand the purpose of anything of this. His laugh is a howl, the devil himself would never make a deal with the Stranger. I am freezing, he tells me I will get used to it. And one day he may allow me to remember, the hairs from the word famous never touched my lips. But there are hairs that are worse that dangled and were fetched and spun into ropes. I pause for a moment, I still feel Love's lips and her last kiss. I now feel the ropes. The unwaking is up at my shoulders and making itself heavy. I wonder if we have much farther to walk. He smiles, we have already traveled miles and have not moved from this spot.

There is little more to see, and if he were to grant me a window I could see it is night. He has already taken me from shelter and brought me to curse. I can join him in an hour, if I would like to rest. I can join him in an hour, and he can teach me how to forget. Restlessness has removed the difference between night and day upon his train, and surrender is at its dinner table, surrender is holding its forks.

We stand at the last door I will be allowed to open, he is going inside to leave me to wonder how he disappeared. He points to the room he has shown me twice, and tells me to return in an hour. He has the strangest smile, we part ways in the corridor, I feel the unwaking in my jaw. I reenter the room with the exquisite table and the exquisite chair. There is clothing upon the bed. There is clock on the wall with two hands that point to the only number. I am alone and about to beg and I will be the only one to hear. This unwaking is mine and all mine and Love is safe from it. Love is far from here with our home wrapped around her. I press my face against the wall, trying to imagine it as her cheek. I will suffer this night and find the strength for four more.

I am quick to dress and then quick to be reluctant to pick up the pen from the table and scratch it across the paper. I was told I am here to bait the waters and call the charms to the surface, and he would feed upon the sugar and the cream. It was his unique vision of a train arriving at unknown stations. I hear him again like a tongue at my ear, a boot on my chest, he demands only the fall of the narrator. Even as I am unwaking, I describe the last perfect moment with Love. Her hair fell aside and the sun asked to be warmed by her smiles. Her eyes glowed to tell my steps to never forget. There is nothing to push, nothing to lose and nothing to steal. We have what can only be ours and the forever things come in piles. I will never forget how beautiful she was, the last time I saw her.

There is a press and a knock upon the door that never closed, the air in the room buckles and my eyes raise to find the Stranger waiting impatiently. The clock is finished, it has spent itself and is dripping down the wall. I have been dressed and brought here. I am in the unwaking and I wish I had never released her hand. I want to consider returning home, I want to speak of all that calls me home. The Stranger tells me we have not arrived, we are in the teeth. He can drag me or I can attempt to walk.

He assures me his fury knows no limits, and his contempt has no ears for pleas or reasons. I am already walking as less of a man as I arrived. His tools have been removed from the walls, and he stands here now with simple heartless motivation. He came back to find me deep in the unwaking. He will be satisfied enough by morning, by morning the narrator will be long vanished and the writer will be slick on the stones. He will be satisfied once he hears the bones and tones and promises breaking, once he listens to the gasps around his creeping hands. I know forever, and he is eternal. His satisfaction is a deepening pool and I will understand the bottom.

The Stranger leads me beyond the historic chopping blocks, he leads me further to a room. He tells me to forget how easily I agreed to come. He tells me to enjoy myself, before tonight becomes tomorrow. I follow him and my legs still feel proud, but this is before they will be forgotten. My legs are still hers, before he takes them. He laughs when I tell the walls my soul will be untouched. I have never met the Stranger, and he tells me he had never encountered a smell like me, and his fingers could not resist a touch of us, and the fall was short in design and long in its hold.

He ushers me into the room, in the aching unwaking. The disappeared tools are gathered about the room. The Stranger has become Strangers. My pride falters into the past, the kiss has become the last. If I withstood his hands, I can not withstand a dozen more. I may as well have some comfort tonight, before they take away all that shifts me and all that may ever wake me. These extra hands, they sit with him, they do his work, they speak in the way he instructs them to speak, they follow his manner and his cunning. They are going to find the soft before they offer him the meat. I will never question why I boarded this train. And every one of their smiling faces will remind me. We raise our glasses and fall into a feast, with a rousing toast that the comfort will quicken into the intolerable.

I realize I am not where I am supposed to be, the unwaking slips into a brief defiance that the Stranger seems to have anticipated with his fingers. They find it, they squeeze seeking not the juice but the grease. I have a want that is calling like a fever. He wants to break the trust that it will ever bring me home. I am sitting in a room filled with seats, a room in which I don't belong. I am pretending to indulge and thinking of what this evening may have been, hours when Love and I may have spoken and held each other, hours which would cave before we grew tired. I am thinking of her walk and her talk as the Strangers raise their glasses again. I am thinking of what they would steal from me. I am thinking of a happier time, the days they want to rip from my arms and my legs and my face. I am battling the unwaking and stepping into the musk and the honey.

'To Johnny,' they make a toast that is like a cough in my eyes. The plates are removed before the meal is half finished and only the glasses are replenished. I thought this was going to be a horribly social affair, but wonder now if it is indeed a business affair. The Strangers mostly keep their backs to me, but I see now they were indeed the tools hanging upon the walls. They creak and they clang just the same. They study me with eyes, but not with eyes like his.

I see within my glass, my drink has changed. It is gone from cold to ice, from less unpleasant to intolerable. It does not chase my senses, it holds them like gravy. The Stranger tells me it is to keep me unwaking, to keep the interests of the others, so they won't forget their shared ambitions. He speaks and he sprays the walls. I want to walk home, and he wants to walk across my back. I want to leap out the window and he refills my glass as he tells me he has already taken it away. He says if it would help me understand, he could take a rib as though it were a long bend in a century.

Or I can lay and drown in a wish I should have never spoken. For the dream to be a writer is a wet one, the dream to be a writer for just one person is something his thirst could not resist. The Stranger says I will taste fame and it will be the fame he feeds me and when my stomach comes up from my insides he will use my shirt as a napkin. It is of no relevance or concern what I wished for was freedom. I don't want to tolerate the way he speaks to me. And he is terribly bored with my freedom. I had it all and couldn't feel the weight. He is going to take a year as his price, a year for a bone, a year for a wish, a year for a regret.

He asks if I suffer the movement of the train beneath my feet. He laughs at my eyes because I couldn't see what I have already given. The Stranger will be satisfied when his price is paid. Another glass for the ride, another glass for the unwelcomed, another glass for the unwaking. I shouldn't worry, the uneasiness will soon change to uncertainty, and soon enough, if I am fortunate, it will be nothing at all. He needs me to split, he needs me in halves and then pieces. I will be another masterpiece. He won't long tolerate the fact he underestimated me, how I can still think and walk while unwaking.

The conversation has gone from buzzing to bristling, and the Stranger now seems to scold the Strangers, and he stands taller for their silence. I have never felt a cloud or a numb quite like this. Before business must come a focus, before conquest must be a focus. He is speaking to everyone in the room and not to me. He is speaking around me. A final toast to my name that will be forgotten, to my face that will never be remembered. To my voice that will never be heard. My glass was drinking blue and now my hand grips it red. A final toast, not among friends or enemies, a final toast, among the Stranger and the Strangers and me. He laughs before I claim my heart and soul will never be his. It is hers. Love will never forget. He quickly refills his glass and all of his glasses.

I know the Stranger has long abandoned any hint of the truth, he drops words in a basket he would have suffer in a desert. To Johnny, as he sits here terrified and alone on this train. I am not terrified, and I would speak if allowed. Still I am here, unwaking, swirling in this capturing room. There is one who will remember me. There is one who wears white and green and red and black and a smile that staggers me from the instance. Hands refill my glass and bring them to my face and my faces. These are my faces of the past, present, and future. These are the caviar beneath his steps, these are the swan and the lamb in his roast.

The Stranger raises his arms and now his hands. He has saved me from the winter, the spring will not spit and the summer will not scorch. He promises a promise that is already broken into splinters. But I believe there is one who remembers, I believe there is one who will count the days and come find me. 'A toast to Johnny Industry,' the Stranger bellows. And the glasses raise and perhaps even mine. The strangers don't care that I may have introduced myself as Leo. That name is lost to all but one. I wonder if she is beneath a blanket and in her chair, I wonder if she is comfortable now. I can not stand or sit, there is nothing but the chains and the locks now, they are louder than the groans of the engines, they are louder than the stealth of the train. 'To Johnny Industry,' he toasts again. The rest comply with their glasses and their eyes come upon me fast, their eyes come searching and angry.

They can not bring themselves to object. The meat does not fit the plate, my legs do not respond. My eyes are fixed upon his glass, my glass, not our glass, my mouth can't twist into words. I can hear, if that is indeed what I do. I can feel, in this unwaking. Love is so far away, I feel her absence. The Stranger moves from where he stands, he parts the bodies, he splits the space, he wants one more crushing look at me. His eyes tell me he believes he is right, his eyes tell me he has never believed himself to be wrong. If I were alone, I may have been a man with a heart impossible to search, I may have been a man with a soul that could not be broken like the rain. But together with Love, we have tight and forever raw seams, together we are a heat too hot to cast into a fire, and our separation is absolutely delicious.

The Stranger tells me it was never weakness, it was willingness, and the trust that tells us we will always come around the fingers of the clock. There will always be another day. My Love will never abandon me. His laughter chokes the air from the room, and all the strangers fall into a heavy pause. The Stranger seems to choose his own words carefully, as if they may fall, as if they won't drag. His teeth are close to my chest, they are at my breath and they remind my legs I won't leave. When she sees what he has done to me, when she realizes all I have forgotten, once she knows all these nights have been smashed by hammers. He is going to make the memories fall as though they fall through fingers. The ache will be gone and the dirt will be gone, the filth will remain and I will have nothing more to keep her.

And if I wonder why again he will take my lips and explain his dances and line the trenches with my hairs. I will never forget, I am starving for her. We will recover from this unwaking. 'To Johnny Industry,' he toasts again, and promises he will hide me in corners she can't find. I cling to thoughts she knows. I can be trampled and blind and deaf. I can be speechless and never cold. I can be trapped and always heard. There is no weight to the wonder. There is no wait to the wonder. The Stranger tells me we are all friends here, he lies to me and tells me we are all friends here. And if Love is not here, where can she be.

I will love her in the moonlight he can not undress, I will love her in the pale days and the damp days and the days that have no particular meaning. I am unwaking and watching his fury grow and unfold. I have been apart from Love for one day and he claims he has already taken three. I have not moved from Love and he claims he can't count the miles we have traveled. Love and I are one in the same, and he offers a box and a match, and a mule to drag us. It is only pressure and time that breaks the human existence. And he will take my teeth if I speak of the forever things again. He points for my glass to be refilled, as if this will remove what I know and dream of, when I am both sleeping and awake.

The Stranger announces to applause this time, 'This is Johnny.' They are going to work through my bones now, they each know what to take. I am in a blizzard and fury of strangers' hands. Each drops their glass and their revelry and their confidence now. They ignore who I am and remember the task. I can not fight or struggle from this unwaking. This is the passion to be destroyed upon this train. This is the passion that calls me home, this is the passion that is the price. My Love, as I feel their hands, I wonder when we will sleep again. As the lines are blurring the Stranger shouts the lie, I asked for fame, and he speaks it again.

He beckons the others closer, they come like a line of clouds, teaching themselves my new name. They spread and speak as though there is no memory of Leo. I reach for a hand I know and the Stranger is amused I believe I will remember. He has already told me he is unburdened by time and space, he walks where and when he chooses and the train is controlled by his will. But if I could just see her soft beautiful face, if I could hear her tempest voice. I would lay in these dogs so she would not, I would lay in her arms at any cost.

I can hear the last song we listened to together and the laughter we shared when I showed her my dance. The strangers are coming upon me like piles of savages, they are coming to shred and find and not to know. I lay in this unwaking, in this terrible terrible mistake. The Stranger declares I have replaced yesterday's man and I can not deny it because no one defies him. He hands me an insisting long drink with a snarled stem and tells me he has taken the center and the warmth. I am in the middle and the others are asking questions I can't hear and they are asking questions with their fingers. I am falling from their reach, and I am barely gone, and asking in the silence for Love to come find me.

The Stranger announces I am gone. I can not defy it, for he is not only the center but the chill within the center. And though I am no more, I want. I want some minutes at Love's cheek, I want some time within her touch. I can be found in the softness, I can be found on a quiet sunny day. I just want to be the man who writes lovenotes to her, I want to be nothing more. In the crush of the closing strangers, I whisper goodnight, to her, I love you, to her. There is only this room within this train and I do not know the hour. I see nothing but her face. I am unwaking, and she is smiling. Perhaps my silent defiance is what makes the Stranger now hold his ribs.

He screams and takes the noise and breath from the air. He smiles through his eyes as though he may wish to devour me and everyone else. The Stranger points at me, he begins speaking in the lowest most despairing tones. This is Johnny Industry, and they all can stop searching through my pockets and my skin. It is not any talent I have that will be used. My voice will not be heard, my visions will not be seen. My devotion will not be felt. I am now Johnny Industry, because his prize will be my will to endure. His prize will be my ultimate failure. The others can and will be satisfied, they can all be made wealthy. And once he his satisfied with the final crumb he will take, the long ride will cease.

I fear this is the last moment I stand, the last I hold. This is the last of my sinking awareness. I am a temporary necessity, I am but another tool to be discarded. I am unwaking, I can barely hear her words, Leo, my Leo. The Stranger boasts he found me like a stray in the yard, I thought our fever had heat, I believed my shadow was separate from his shadow. He is pressing his intentions as though I can not hear or refuse.

This is Johnny Industry. He is a splash in the face of humanity, he is the wash and wax into its eye, he is the fingers pushed into its mouth. They are separating me into ideas and glimpses and uses and piles and not talents. They are separating me into pieces and not promises. Because even in this state my will remains until it is broken. The Stranger arouses the strangers to bring them to silence. This is Johnny Industry, this is the cruelest of tricks. I am being measured and mapped, I am being divided and bargained for. I am being claimed and resold.

I wait for the numbness he speaks of, I am waiting for the surrender I can not escape. This is the first of five nights to endure. I amuse him, he growls, he may keep me. I entertain him, believing the start has not already swelled into the finish. Where is my Love? It is but my will that has brought me through the first three stolen nights, it is my will that leaves me standing against the unwaking. They are all talking like maggots crawling to a meal. I can see her face. I can't unfeel, I can't forget. Tonight grows into a darkness, it is a choice and I don't belong. I hope Love can not follow me here, and I hope Love can find me. I feel as the confusion and the betrayal no longer seek the weakness, they become more monsters in the room.

The Stranger has the scent of blood in his teeth, and the retreating strangers are invited to come back away from the walls and the corners in which they hide. This is Johnny Industry, the coming flash, the inevitable flame. The brilliant loose sensation, the empty spectacle to feed the starving. I am being escorted, or carried. There is an eagerness about, there is whispering among the ghost voices. There are chains and wires and tubes, I hear hammers and nails. There are two sets of eyes in every conversation, those that are watching and mine which are struggling to remain open. Those that are in control and mine that are closing fast.

If my bed was not miles from here, I would be sleeping. If my bed were not miles from here, I wouldn't have come. I hear their objections. I am still too loose for the eyes, I am a hair against a tongue, I am still too salty to the taste. I am still somewhere still conscious and thinking and aware. The Stranger's face appears in the pool. I have given him no choice but to hang the chains of a fourth night around me, he is going to wrap them tight at the neck and heavy upon the shoulders. I need only nod, to show him I understand. I have to accept nothing, but he can continue the lie longer than I can withstand. He can manipulate beyond the breaths I may steal. I must realize by now he has never failed and he has never been endured. The want he sees in my eyes is surprising and exquisite.

'So much struggle from a forgotten man,' the Stranger says. He has three thumbs on each hand to take care of such things. The others are awaiting their turns like darlings in a candy shop. I am undeniably in their hands, I haven't an idea of the last I moved of my will. But it is his hands I should loathe, his hands I should fear. He holds me like a liquid, he holds me like the unwaking and the unescaped. He wants me to remember, he is giving me everything I never asked for. And one day he may tire of me and make a truce with me. If I forget the precious quiet days and the beautiful nights, I can wear the chains and forget the day I boarded his train. He will offer me a version of the truth I can learn to sleep beneath. I can earn a chance to not cry out with regret.

I need only surrender my will and accept I wanted this, before he reaches the end of his patience. I am the mess and the wreck and the tatters, brought to the room that was never to be entered. I am to fill this empty room, Johnny Industry will be the darkness that finds every inch and corner, Johnny Industry will be the laughing light.

'I took your name,' the Stranger says. And I will fill this room with unasked fame, I will fill this room until I disappear. I will be meat on a table, and a promise I never made. I will be meat on a table, and a dream I never had, a wish I never wished, and the Stranger's lost coal of ambition and trickery. I will be released before my gentle hands regain themselves. I will be released before my gentle heart can apologize. He is going to use the words I was never able to speak.

He will give fame but I will have long slipped beneath the unwaking and I will never see the stars. The Stranger drops in one more close looping sniff, and maybe I will forgive myself, and maybe I will believe, she pulled her blanket tight before she could ever hear the words I could never find. He tells me that in the centuries he has lived, the centuries that have survived him so far, he has never known a narrator to slip out of his skin like a snake. But he is all too happy to show me the way, and to show me how to dance happier to a day without a sunrise.

I am but a drop in the unwaking, too far from Love to speak. I am too far from her to hear, too far from her to feel. I hope my legs aren't cold tonight, they curl around themselves. I hope I am not too cold tonight, I would love to find my way home.

TABLE

I dangerously dreamed, I will call it last night, knowing my thoughts are no longer safely kept in boxes. I remembered Love can tempt me in any color, I hunt for her in every fragrance.

I dreamed of the first time I saw Love wear red, and my mouth smiled like the gentleman who will never speak of it. I dared without being conscious of doing so. I dreamed she blew her cool remedies upon me. The Stranger promises to drape fifteen more nights upon me. My eyes are no longer allowed to close, I am ruined beyond any pain I may receive. I dreamed and I was aware I am unable to keep secrets. I secretly hoped Love was searching for me, and she would not find me here. I can not bear the thought of her in this place.

I can not feel the days the Stranger has claimed. I feel the red, somehow, and her skin that was mine. I can feel the table, it has long come to know me and devour me. It has become my corner of the world. I am seated before it, I am bent awkwardly forward, I fail as though the Stranger chose to take my spine before my will. The table's surface is smooth and no longer indifferent to me, my face is upon it like paint. When he took my spine he took the strength from my neck. When he took my voice, he did not take Love's name from my lips.

I do not know and would not remember if the machine upon the table was placed or if it grew. It is part of the grand illusion he has chosen, the illusion I was cast into. My hands are always upon the machine. The machine is a typewriter and its teeth are in my fingers. If there is silence or a pause I can hear the whispers, 'It will keep its fingers here and it will keep its fingers moving.'

The table has my legs, it is my legs. I would fall without it and it would lean without me. We are not walking, we are not leaving, we are not sleeping. We are together without a hope of escape. My eyes are open in an angry gash of wakefulness. But I can feel more than I can actually see. I can feel my captivity. I can feel the room and its far reach and its closing reach.

Perhaps I was told, or I simply understand now. I am Johnny Industry. We are Johnny Industry. I never asked for it, I never aspired to it. I am in the Stranger's arms. They reached and were accepted freely and they can not be unspread or unfelt. They block time, they block day and night. I have no control. There are hands upon my hands, there are hands in my mind, there are hands that cover my mouth. I have been told, I do not yet understand. This is no trick. The Stranger speaks, tapping a finger upon my forehead. I am we, I have ceased to be, he has erased me like a smear. We are the burst, we are the relentless train. We are Johnny Industry, we are the unthinkable and the easy, we are the unforgettable and the unforgiveable.

The Stranger will defy reality, it is his way and it is his talent. It is his slow drag. He tells me I should open my eyes, he insists I see how human will pales beside him. I lost the will when I stepped away from her. A predator does not seek the weakest, he finds the one who is unknowingly alone. If I have not been sleeping and not been dreaming, if I am not awake and aware, I ask him to tell me where I have been taken. 'Yes,' he answers. I recoil without the freedom of movement, and the Stranger searches me for cracks and strain.

He steps into the silence and the darkness he has created. He controls the light. He controls the truth. I will trade him submission for a moment's peace. I should open my eyes and see what hunger wears and see how it walks. The Stranger's smile returns to yellow when I agree to admit to whatever he says. If I could find myself in a garden, if I could find myself where I belong. He sneers and speaks as though he is holding me behind his eyes.

Those tears were wept some time ago. It isn't the sunlight in my eyes that make things difficult to see.

We are Johnny Industry. The other strangers have faces and voices that are no more than his expressions and his range of tone. The train continues and plows relentlessly forward, it slips through empty hours and stops only to feed. We are Johnny Industry. We are an onslaught upon the senses, we are overwhelming, we are an uncomfortable taste, we are empty and confusing and impossible to ignore.

The Stranger is but one and appears as many. There are the new and the greedy, the cruel and the indifferent, those who have joined the party and those who wait on the tracks. I am but the empty vessel, my hands remain in the machine. The rest is the will and the illusion of the exotic Stranger.

We are Johnny Industry. There is one who sings the songs I can not write, another to perform the dances I can not follow. Another sculpts and paints murals to suffer upon the towns we pass. One speaks in smoky poetry in a language I can not recite, another hovers around my shoulders and plays instruments I can not pronounce. Every word and every image is a step, a press, a force, a crush.

It will not make him stop speaking but I tell him, yes, yes my eyes are open. I can see it. This place is what he has chosen to make it, it is the reality he can refold and undress. The strangers are faces that provide an empty noise. They are the fog that looks like fame. I am Johnny Industry, and he will demand the moment I possess, and the moment I will lose, as the most famous person alive. I am Johnny Industry and I hang onto dust. My mind betrays me, my lips still spill secrets. He took the last thing I saw, and my hopes and dreams will follow.

The Stranger reveals the magazine covers, the stumbling interviews, the midnight shows. The fame I never desired is growing in ten second flashes, in an avalanche of fantasy. The world can not admit I am impossible, because one elbow touches the next, one delight must become another delight. He tells me the rocks have already begun to roll down the hillside and everyone is too blind to see it coming. All they can see is the train approaching upon the tracks. No one can resist the irresistible.

The Stranger is certain I can feel everything, the moving train, the blinding lights, the inevitability. The luxury of this room, the hold of my prison, the freedom of my fame. I am Johnny Industry. We are Johnny Industry. The most famous fruit in a fleeting hour. He crawls about, not with hands and knees, but with his words. He crawls about, searching me. He spreads another spill, he spreads another doubt. If I asked him for a teacup, he has given me a sword. If I asked him to speak of the beauty of Love, he will remind me I begged to drown in the mud.

He reminds me he will never barter, and I am less than a fool if I take him at his word. I gave him an hour and he has taken my days. I should have remained still, and ignorant, I should have been patient and waited. Because now he brushes the promises and brushes the paints. He has my fingers answering questions I never asked. He is going to touch the things I won't allow to be touched.

I will endure the endless to keep the forever. 'There is no one here to say goodnight to you, Johnny,' the Stranger says. He can offer tomorrow like a pill, or tomorrow like a take. My eyes are open and he can show me the faces who know my name. He has thickened the fog, and I have been taken from the vine. The Stranger tells me has given me a name to be forgotten. He will pull and pick at a name until it is forgotten. He can first show me the fame I never desired.

My eyes are open and finally see the silence and the room is empty once again. I want to see a dream, my eyes are wet with the hope for a dream. I want to see something beyond the machine and the table and the monstrosity I have become. I want a night in which I won't answer to the name I have been given. I lay here shivering in what was made by lovers. I am trying to breathe its air. I lay long upon this table of fame and shame.

I remember the stars and the moon, and I wonder where Love is at this very moment. The Stranger has laid us in cold corners of an inseparable world, I long to see our gardens, I long to see her kiss, I long to see the cling and deep clutch. I am in the hold of a hole, so far from my promises. I wish I could speak and tell her where I am and I want to be found. The table embraces a little closer, a little tighter, I feel its weight remove my own.

I sense the cold and sense the storms coming about, they are all around, and I risk a breath. I was the happiest man alive. I long to be called Leo, once more. The storms will forget me, the faces that named me will forget me. I lay still as can be, aching to be called Leo. In someone else's darkness, I will refuse to be torn and refuse to be turned. The train is barreling recklessly through the silence and the sickness. The next day and the next town are waiting for Johnny Industry. They are waiting for the cleverness, waiting for the shock and dismay. They are waiting as though they can not help itself. The Stranger says the train is coming to occupy the empty spaces.

My heart is in my mouth, my hands are in the machine, there is a shadow across my shoulders, and I try to believe my soul is beyond this room. I am dreaming I am sawing the table into pieces and Love stops me before I fall into the winds. She wants to show me a first anticipated kiss, and then a second, she wants to show me the eyes and the look that hopelessly stole me. I can not be taken again. I am possessed and I am hers in the softest of surrenders. I am hers to keep because I had never been. For however long I have been away, I dream recklessly. I dream of the forever things, with her hands at my waist, her eyes at my will, her legs across mine. We are in a dance of the winged.

The Stranger stands close enough I feel him within me. I will be broken and the pieces sold, I feel his words like tiny tacks across my skin. I will be sliced like cake and sold as Johnny Industry. I will be soaked before he puts me in the fire. It doesn't matter that I can no longer be trusted in the darkness. I was a vulnerable fool for wanting more. It is too late, his train owns the day and owns the night. I asked for nothing and he is giving me more, in exchange for taking everything. I will never understand, and I will wish to forget. My fingers are moving and heaving, they are aching in the machine, and the Stranger can hear every word, and I hear nothing beyond his voice.

The Stranger has his finger in my ear. Love is not coming for me. He drove me to lost and then covered the trail. I vanished beyond a memory, I am sinking in caves, the dogs can't find me and the hunt can't find me and the want can't find me. He spits the word Leo on the ground and only the flies find it. My eyes are open, and he tells me what I will see. In a week I will be the most famous name on the planet. 'Look at yourself and see what she will see,' the Stranger says. I must open my eyes and see all he is given and all he has taken. His mouth comes close again, he wants me to scream and cry, he wants me to wish I was on the tracks and not in the train.

He tells me comfort is an illusion, and Love will not wish to be near me again. There is no love so blinding or forgiving. The Stranger wants me to remember. I wanted to be a writer, because the narrator hovered so close he could nearly taste the words. The narrator was choking and fumbling. But he will make certain she hears and sees every word, every word I never found, every word that was beyond. 'Love will find me, it will only be five days,' I say. He puts a boot upon my legs and leaves it there. He tells me he has long since taken that, and times over and over. He asks if I can taste the miles at his heels. He can travel to always in a day. He can walk a year in a breath. The reward is nearly too sweet for his lips, nearly, but not completely. It is an unexpected pleasure that he keeps like a cobweb. 'Love is alone and angry now, Johnny,' he says. And he tells me of the lies I have spoken.

I have never spoke a lie to Love. There has never been one in my mind or my heart. I feel ravaged and hopeful and the Stranger reminds me I am his possession for as long as he feels comfortable wearing this suit. For as long as he is entertained. He will be satisfied when I am forgotten. Just as he was forgotten. But it will be in no mean or manner or shape as delicious. I will be famous. I will not reappear. I will be famous in the scent and shape he creates, and I will never resurface. 'You are going to want to forget me like the dangle of candy,' he says. But the Stranger will be at the throat of the days.

He tells me Love's hands and her hold haven't disappeared, but my eyes will never again close. She will live to forgive and I will watch her long regret. The Stranger's words are promises to himself, only he truly understands them. He wants me to know, anything and everything in the world is a short drip from his face into his stomach. My head is between his hands, and it would be too simple to crush. He wants me to see my last dream, and know it could be within the train's next bend or crossed bridge. He is bringing me to heights to enjoy the fall, and then he will pick me from his teeth and walk away.

'I will forget you, Johnny,' he says. He will forget me first, it is his earned right and privilege. And the rest of the world will forget me, and that will be the slowest drain. He tells me we have traveled for seven days, and now he tells me we have traveled for twelve. Somehow I refuse to hear with my eyes open and my mouth open to his words. Because I can see Love and I feel her kiss.

He has made me the pathetic writer I wished to be, and she will hear all those words which escaped me. She will hear every word that was meant for her, and so will everyone else. There seems to be twelve of him, the Stranger, within the arms of this room, in the dance of this room. I am the food left for the feast. I am in his impossible shadow, I am his creation. And when he took me, he took us. 'You are Johnny Industry,' he says. He wants me to say it, and feel it.

Now that I am in his hands, as the Stranger casts me about, as he doubles me over, as he uses me to sweep the floors, as he casts me like a sweeping lead net. I am a wonder and a monster, I am a finger in the eyes, an assault upon the senses. I am spreading and the world goes to sleep without knowing where they will wake. The pieces are growing and spreading and the hiding places are being discovered. Johnny Industry is a name that is growing like a plague, it is being spoken in the streets, it is a sneeze across the screens, it is a shadow against the windows, it is a gurgle in the alleys.

I will be pressed into the public's faces. They will be forced to understand. I am not a man, I am a machine. I am the industry and the Stranger peddles his product. The purity and sensibility are removed, the romance and honesty are removed, the passion is removed. He took a face he despised, and now he has given me a face I will not recognize. I am a lick that is no longer wet. The people are watching, and they are listening. They are asking for more when they don't understand. The Stranger wants me to feel the seclusion.

The Stranger tells me how many days it has taken, to make me not believe all that I see. I cling to my secret thoughts. Love is here, I feel her in the stillness. No, no he says, he has washed her from me, from elbow to knee, from ear to toe, and she chooses to remain just where she is, untouched and unharmed and far from me. I don't trust the truths he speaks from different sides of his mouth, I don't trust the places they take me. He isn't burdened by the truth, he doesn't carry its weight. He tells me to count his slick steps across the floor, and he offers tomorrow in exchange for untouchable years.

I wouldn't mind the burn of his exaggeration if I could slide onto the feel of Love's soft cheek. He is gone now, he vanished like the Stranger. This is my silence, this is my darkness. It will not be shared, it is all I feel. I want to speak, my own voice has become so unfamiliar. I wait for the will to move, and then I begin to search for the will. Move first to straighten, move next to stretch and stand. I tell myself in the silence, I can no longer accept the impossible. The long days from home did not exist and can not exist. I will listen to no more of the treachery. I will no longer see what I am given, I will again see what is here. If I can't leave voluntarily, I will escape. I will be with Love, I ache for her voice.

I strain for the comfort and the words, I try to tell myself, this is all a dream and one that has transpired in a single night. The journey has been but a mile, and Love was never lost, and we were never alone.

The doors are closed and the windows are gone and the lights have left to be friends of another. I will stand. Leaving begins with the first determined step. My head has become an enormous weight, my neck and shoulders feel the pull. This table my face has endured seems reluctant to release me. In the darkness we battle, I gain an inch, and now another. My unsteady head is like a boulder. And my hands feel helpless and so far down my arms. I count them, I have one, and then two. I am willing them to move, willing them to help. Three fingers of a hand are being worked through jaws, as are two of the other. If I can gain my hands I can find my face, my eyes, my mouth, my ears. I have all night to accomplish this, and I will leave freely in the morning. I will rediscover the reality, the Stranger has no hold upon me.

My arms are impossibly weak and impossibly long. My back will not straighten. It does not pain me, it does not refuse. It is frozen in a twist. I remember my legs. One feels as though it is bone against ungiving wood. I move it an inch and the table groans and breaks the silence. The other is lost behind me, stretched until my foot touches the wall. I hear the Stranger whisper this is the wait before morning. The dark will bleed from black to brown to gray. He will allow my self pity and denial, he will allow me to convince myself I have only been here one day. My reality means nothing now, my belief can not be heard.

The Stranger returns, and all the strangers are here. He dances about in the light, he is a piece of us all we should never dare eat. He holds the warm midsection of a lie upon the table, where my head was trapped just hours before. He gives me permission to see and hear, to speak and even scream. It doesn't matter now. Today is his creation and yesterday is gone. Today offers no promises or gifts, it offers no forgiveness or freedom. He can paint it across my eyes, he can erase it. There is nothing to gain in struggle. No relief will exist between what was taken and what now possesses me.

The Stranger has come to explain, and there is no reason for me to understand. The man who was named Leo is not in a hole, he is not a prisoner behind bars, he is not hidden in a box, he wasn't stolen by the dogs. He is not a victim. Leo is a name that has no sweetness. 'You are nearly famous, now, Johnny Industry,' he says. Fame is an empty word and not one of my desires. And fame is now mine. He demands I see all they have done for me, and he does not care if I believe it. He demands I see all they have done to me, and he does not care if I accept it.

The Stranger's grip can't be forced to release. It is iron and ecstasy and puzzling. Johnny Industry has been pushed like a numbing fist into the consuming faces. They wonder where the wind came from and how they may follow it. They drink beyond thirst, they devour beyond hunger. They stand upon their heads and walk with their hands. The Stranger is orchestrating the curiosity and he is redirecting the confusion. He is manipulating the objection. I am Johnny Industry, we are Johnny Industry, by his will and his hands. I am the mystery, the unseen and the unheard, and he is feeding the cattle and growing the herd and leading the march into the fire.

I am the source, I am his creation. The strangers wear different faces and carry only my name. They arrived like a flood, they arrived like a storm. The Stranger tells me, 'It is not me. It is you.' He glistens, because he is unforgettable, he glows because he is not forgotten. Johnny Industry is waiting and lurking behind every empty song, every image that is dismissed and then embraced. I am a quote, I am a ringtone. I was first eleven different faces, and then I became seventeen. I have been everywhere, and I am nowhere to be found.

Because the impossible can be made possible with but a flex of the Stranger's strength. It will all be remembered, only to be forgotten. The purpose is to deceive and lure, to bake and frenzy and disappoint, to create an empty hysteria and then vanish. The Stranger reaches suffering to all, not just to me. It is the walk he has had, from the beginning, it is the only walk he will know. He wants curiosity, and then belief. He wants people to form lines, he wants them in a madness, in a blinding shuffle. He wants the anticipation to rise like pain. He wants desire to become an empty need, a curse, an itch.

I am the name he has given me, I am the faces he has given me. I am no more than the price he has chosen. So the Stranger can exist in the darkness and lurk in the unknown, so he can hide behind the curtain and appear from beneath the rug. It is true, I never wanted any of this, and I will never remember what I asked for.

I wondered if there could be something more. And I spoke it aloud in front of his teeth and I spoke it aloud in the company of his cold. I had a face and a name that possessed a beautiful lover. Ours was a truth that could never have been touched. It was never defenseless before he took it. We were never fragile and he found no weakness. There was to be no interruption and there was to be no end. The Stranger appears and disappears, he loathes that he is forgotten and labors to be forgotten. He is the distraction and the parade and the fire that burns it all to ash.

'Johnny, I will take and not ask for another bite,' he says. Leo is the name that is no longer spoken, he became what he would never become. And now Love is just Love, and he has taken two bites and eaten two hopes. I will look in the mirror and understand I do not want to see my face against hers again. I will never, I will never, and he tells me I will beg him to let me stay. I will ask to be hidden, I will ask to learn to appear from the darkness. The Stranger wishes nothing but the best for us, we are simplicity that breathed and conquered, we are a choke at the back of his throat. He wants us to be forever, but we are but a wrinkle in his coat, a dog to be kicked aside, a passion he can not extinguish.

He holds a muddy puddle in his hands that he will shape into a mirror. I can feel how monstrous I have become. He insists I see the face I now wear, the one she will not recognize, the one she will never tolerate. The face that will chase her screaming. He reminds me, he is granting me fame for the price of a kiss, the last kiss I will never receive. The Stranger gives the never wished for, his giving is filthy, he steals what can not be stolen. It is an intolerable blanket, a humming in the nights. There is a light behind my eyes that feels like tears. There is a breath that refuses me. I face the mirror and look upon what I could never be and what Love can never see. His price will be all I do not remember and all I can not forget.

Love's beautiful face is in my mind, and I refuse to picture it beside my own face. I can see not what I wanted, only what I have become. The Stranger licks his lips before he calls me horrible. I recoil from myself, I am something nightmares flee. My head must be six times its size, it twists above the strain and struggle of my neck. My arms are twice as long as they were and folded gruesomely backwards upon themselves. My hands have but nuggets remaining as fingers and the rest are within the machine, they are swallowed and typing even now, when I am not looking and when I ask them to stop. In his mirror I must be at least eleven feet in length, or more, and the Stranger is laughing. He picks some of my last hairs from the floor and places them back on my head. The remaining hairs are wisps that fall down my shoulders and back. I find my legs, they are beneath me, they are in front of me and behind me. One is enormous and one is nearly bone, and I can not see where my legs end and the table begins.

The Stranger spits the word escape, and he spits it again, he blows the word hope from his nose, and he steps in it. And all the while my fingers are working and I feel the pulsing and I wonder if I am indeed creating all of this myself. I can see tubes coming from the feeding machine, they are filling with slow lazy climbing oil, the tubes run thick to the ceiling and across the floor. In his mirror I see the chains drop into sight and fall upon me and watch as they retreat back to where they came.

He will not allow me to ask what I have become. 'You are Johnny Industry.' I am famous and now Love hears the words I was never able to speak. The world sees me and hears me as he has fashioned and imagined. Until he decides I will cease as though I never existed. Leo is gone and soon Johnny will follow. I will be kept behind a curtain, I will be kept in the stench. I am a vessel to a purpose. An idea that should never have been born. I will remember what I asked for.

My eyes are horrified and I am speechless. I never asked the Stranger for anything, but I will beg now. I will beg for Love not to come. I want to beg for a large enough shadow, a large enough cage. I want to beg the train to move faster and never stop. 'Don't let her find me,' I say. And the Stranger promises she will. She is going to find me with every one of these inches and every one of these twists, she is going to find me farthest from who I ever was. And this is how I will offer her every perfect word in every perfect way. After I am famous and forgotten, Love will be the only one who remembers. I beg loud enough for the Stranger to hear and for him to laugh and hunger. I fill the room with it, I seep with it. The floor is angry and wet with it, and the Stranger dances in it.

They remove the chains because I am to be famous. It is a fire to be felt, it has already burned, it is coming and building, it is smoke filling the cold. There is no escape. I press against his mirrors. The Stranger watches as I try to find my own eyes. Isn't it glorious, Johnny. He has given everything, everything I could have never imagined, everything I never asked for. I am a rocket, I am a flame, I am unstoppable until the sudden end. He promises the end will bring the bitter silence. The end will allow the tears to flow. Not even Love will come for me, he has made me such a beautiful unspeakable horror. All of this is his. I can not step out of the wind or the wound. If he gathers me in his arms, I can finally again be awake. He wants to see how I find the nights now, he asks if they are still miracles and dreams.

I don't understand why this all had to be. He speaks as though remembering what I said. This is the violation of fame. I said none of this. And yet the train rolls forward, and no night or day can keep it. Perhaps he will find the mercy, he may allow me to lay upon the tracks. I wonder why my fingers continue typing. He tells me it is because I have no courage. My fingers possess meaningless and frivolous movements, nothing more. It is part of the illusion. The Stranger possesses the rest and will never be questioned. He does not need to be followed and he can not be bargained with.

He possesses and he does not need my surrender. He can not be outrun or outnumbered. He brought himself to me, step after step, and it does not matter that I do not remember, I allowed him to come inside. That is when I fell, that is when I won and lost. He tells me to take a longer look in the mirror before he turns out the lights. I can not crawl and I can not beg. I am searching for my eyes and I won't find them here. He has taken what he needed and the rest can not be found on this train. The other strangers will handle the rest and they will claim what is theirs. 'She will never find you and soon you won't remember why,' he says.

It is but another lie to set the world into a spin and a roll across me. I lay still in the crush and he tells me the tears I find will not help. We may have survived the five days, if that were indeed all it was. We may have nearly recovered, had he not taken exactly what he wanted. The Stranger wears a sudden hat and tells me I am just a stripe in the gloom, and he hasn't known pity's or sympathy's legs in many years.

If he allowed me to ask, he would not explain, because the terror of the loss would not keep. It would fall from me, in time, it would fall from me like hair or youth. He again calls me, Johnny Industry, the man who would have nothing at all. He wants to be forgotten, he has always been forgotten, in his own way, in the way that the memory is scorched and unhealed. The Stranger admits, he forced the first two steps, he was up to my chest and forehead before I realized. But I stepped onto his train, and now I am countless miles from home. And he is going to show me a dark sleep does not know.

I attempt to offer him a look of surrender, though I know he is not fooled. I would take a dark with no rest if he would only stop speaking. He tells me again, I have nearly served my purpose. And if my desire was truly to have my words sing to her, then I have truly failed. The success of the Stranger is failure, the goal was always loss. He spoke quite clearly while I longed to hear what I wanted to hear. He spoke with simple words and razor lips, he reminds me it wasn't Tuesday and it wasn't two in the afternoon, and there were no birds about and the flowers dropped their dresses. When he told me the courage of my love was something he wished had no place in this world. It was something he wanted to strangle from the throat of time. He told me people taste better in pieces, they fall in piles when they are in pieces.

'One day you will remember,' he says. I put the hood on myself, I fell under the axe, and Love threw the permission. I will never lie and be heard by the liars. The Stranger smiles, because my eyes just flashed true, he smiles because true does no harm behind his walls. A little hope can be allowed, a little useless hope can be overlooked. He wants me to say the words. I am Johnny Industry. And I don't know how horrible he will allow me to become.

All he has created, the name he wrung through his hands and threw into the world, the grand facade around the aching name. It is all just a brutal sudden flash, after all, it is not inconvenient to him at all. The Stranger brushed around the time he has spent and has barely left his own path. And together they have succeeded, we have succeeded, with no help from me, to find the soft places, the inconsolable spaces. I am a fire with no heat. I am a ten minute interest, a passing glance, a light meal with a forgotten flavor. He tells me he comes across someone like me about once in a century. And it matters little to him because he eludes everything, including wisdom and death.

He tells me I should have been listening. I am an offering to the masses, I am stretched so thin I am nearly transparent. He can see through the paper as easily as he sees through my skin. 'You haven't the weight to keep her, now,' he says, 'you have given up what would hold her.' My Love sought and believed in the light, she awaited the thick reveal, she cherished the truth. It is a watery, lukewarm mess now, we are chasing it with spoons. I am this disgusting thing in a train and she will be the most disappointed. He smiles, because the first thing I freely gave was home. The rest he took before I could object.

The lights will be torn away tonight as though they will never again be seen. He is going to leaving me in the wash. Once I feel and admit I am gone, I will ache for the return. The Stranger can always find one person, there is always one. Someone in the moonlight, someone who feels they are safe, someone who believes more in what they had than what they lost. The Stranger whispers. He never even wore his gloves, and he never took them off. He raked through the beauty, there was no mob to chase him away, there was no safety. Tonight he will leave one light burning, to make me afraid of the dark. He will leave one light burning, to be certain I don't believe I remember.   I look into his eyes and feel the chill and try to convince him I can no longer feel myself. I no longer know myself. What was that name before. I have a wish that is a cry into the silence. He smiles in a twist of happiness. He can step off this train at any moment, and I will be cast off in a heap. The Stranger assures me I am lost, I am a wreckage.

The days are beginning to thin, and he has already finished what he started. Because no man, least of all me, will ever understand the way the Stranger moves between time and shadow and tuck and riddle. 'We grow tired of the meat left on your bones,' he says. He tells me I will never know the reason, but I will know the sweetness of the unrecoverable. I wonder if I might be granted but a single dream, a fleeting dream should do no harm, to retain a piece, and hold it in the morning. He tells me I am Johnny Industry, I was unknown a week ago, and I will be forgotten a week from now, my face no longer has a mouth to hold a dream. I am rising towards the exquisite crash. It has already been set. I have no need for dreams or worries. I should feel my face upon this table, and even that matters little.

He has already written and rewritten what has happened. He will leave me with a rawness at the end of my nose, an itch at my ear I can not scratch. It is the kissless kiss, the reachless reach. And that should bring me through my thoughts tonight. The train and table are the reality and it wouldn't matter if I no longer believe in him. My head is nearly falling from my neck, I feel the pain of my teeth growing and my hair falling from its roots. My shoulders spread wider and my elbows collapse into the wood beneath them.

The Stranger has spent my next days, they have already passed. My hips groan as they stretch further, as the table melts further into me. The hour is growing later and he has tired of my company and he has never enjoyed my company. He took from all the words I have never spoken and given me what I never asked. I do not remember, as he repeats, he found them in my chest, he stole them from my throat, on that damp quiet afternoon, when I was sleeping as though I were safe and alone. It was my fault, I did not hear the doors slam closed behind me. Love told me something had come inside. My eyes were too loose in the paradise.

The coming days will be marvelous, he tells me. I will have everything and lose it all in a moment. And he will disappear and never be seen again. Until he is. That is the ruse and that is the chosen wound. He is going to tell me, he comes unbearably close to my ear, and he opens and closes it. The voice I wanted has reached the masses, and neither Love or I can hear it. The voice is tearing out my guts until I am empty. I have a public now, I have a demand, I am giving her the words she would never hear. And all I used to say aloud in the night is silent, and all that I found in the morning is silent. This is the more, this is the possibilities, this is the could beyond the sweet circle. I had a heaven I would have given up for the love of one woman. It is all within his hands, waiting for a wet clap.

I can feel myself dripping, I can feel myself becoming more monstrous. I am just another small piece he has claimed. The chains are going to drag and become heavier and they are growing locks between their links, and he will walk, lighter than ever. He has granted what follows me, it is so small, and just as Leo has been lost to Johnny Industry, nothing will survive the wind and the wood. Not the train, not the memories.

PURSUIT

In the slow chaos that refuses to move, I believe. In the turmoil that now chooses to be tender, I believe. I listen for the words that were impossible to speak. I'll pursue them in the dark. The dogs are wild for a hunt, eager for a hunt. The Stranger left them with a purpose. He whispered do not let him sleep. There will be no dreams tonight. The dogs ache for me to will myself into an escape. The chains are upon me, working their voices into me, they drag me longer across the floor, longer across the table. They are to leave traces of a man within the monster.

Denied sleep and denied dreams, I am left to secretly, silently believe. If I keep my eyes closed, perhaps they will not know. But the angry bite is something I will see. I look from my arms to my legs to an empty space on the wall. I will believe with eyes opened. I've seen it in the dreams that are not allowed. I've tasted it when I have had thirst and no water. I've tasted it when I have had chains and no bread.

I believe in Love's pursuit. I believe her eyes opened in the heavy waking of the first morning. She knew this was impossible, she knew this could not be. There is no end to color the endless. Her hands would never release me to the dirt or to the Stranger. Her pursuit began before the Stranger boasted. He held his hands wide and proclaimed with his teeth, he was going to take first the days, as many as he wished. He could take seasons, he could take our names and take our denial. I believe I feel her pursuit, whether by car or ship or plane. Love is coming through the whips of the cold, Love is coming through the traps. She is following, she is chasing, she is closing like a storm. She is burning through the foam of the lies, she is pursuing through the endless night. I hope her steps can be heard, I hope they hear her wailing.

Love is a force, I feel her in the room, closer than the chains, closer than the bite of the dogs. She is coming, she is already here. She is all that can not be unfelt, all that can not be refused. I remember. She pressed her lips and she spoke first, she

101

gave me her lover's name. She is bringing the years and the lifetimes and the memories. I must only tolerate a little more of the intolerable, shiver but a little longer in the shade.

The Stranger's voice begins to growl from behind a distance, 'Let her come,' he says. And now he is speaking close at my ear. She knows it is already too late, I was lost with my first step onto the train. His will is heavier than the unimaginable, he has already forgotten the strangers who serve him and the train and the masses who could not resist him. He removes his hat and shows me his mind. Love is safer than a dream, safer than a kiss. I believe the pursuit is growing faster.

He removes his boot from my mouth. I can feed upon whatever I wish tonight, but I will be aware of the stretching, the dragging, I will taste every inch. I hear Love's voice like a song, and he tells me there is no music in his will. There is only devastation. If I would like, he will tell me the story of the pursuit, for it has already been written and finished. The Stranger can tell me the story and use two voices, he can speak in two tongues, he can speak in love and loss.

The first moment she heard the name Johnny Industry, she cried out the name I will never hear again. The Stranger speaks in her voice, 'Those weren't your words, my Leo, I couldn't feel you.' She is coming, through the ice and his poison. He tells me she will find only what he stole and now possesses, she will find only what he leaves behind. He tells me I will see in the light, I will see what I can not deny and already feel. The hopelessness is larger than this room, and Leo is no longer. He can tell me the story of her pursuit, and how she lost against his timeless will.

If I hadn't boarded the train, she may have saved me and saved us. He admits, Love was clever enough to discover the trail, and he was mistaken when he thought the fog would prove to be too thick. She was coming, screaming I was never lost, she was bringing the forever things. The train entered the tunnel heading south, and the Stranger's hand twisted the tunnel and turned the mountain to the west. It was hardly an effort, and he eluded her, we eluded her once, and once was all it took.

After, it was easy to blind her with the snow, it is easy to blind someone who is searching for only one thing. He tells me lovers are the simplest, especially lovers so raw and true. Lovers like us have no chance beneath his boots. In a different twist of circumstance, he might have admired her pursuit. Her passionate search for two days, it may as well have been two hundred years.

Forever can not withstand what he has done, forever can not understand what he has done. And passion is but an afterthought, it is at his whim and pleasure, or displeasure. I believe in Love's pursuit, and he never doubted she would appear again, he anticipated it. The Stranger may have actually appreciated the fever of it all, had he not pushed us through the mechanical twists.

I feel Love's pursuit like the air in the room. The Stranger tells me I will forget what can not be forgiven. He asks if I did not feel every turn, if I did not feel the crush of every hour and mile. When he changes a face and devours a dream, he is a curse that can't be swallowed, he is a spiral that can't be fled. Love is my force, and she was not the slightest challenge. He shows me his pocket watch and tells me she was late. He has already rewritten us, he has already unnamed us. He tells me to feel the hunger and the licking, he is about to truly show me what I have become. This will be the first nightmare he provides and the last I will remember.

Love was horrified by the words and she will be horrified by their source.

This is the freedom he has manufactured and granted, this is the freedom he creates and denies. This is freedom suffering the appetite of fame. His will twisted one into the other. What I asked and what I said never mattered. The humming and the hammering are in my bones, every bone he has removed and sharpened and reshaped. The Stranger has used me. Every inch of me. He has won and he always will. 'Feel her pursuit like the pulse in your neck, Johnny,' he says.

I am the crumble into a collapse that had no purpose. None of this has value or meaning. When he is ready, the Stranger will allow us to return to what we had and what we lost. And she is rushing to save what can not be saved. And his fingers are already gone, they have discovered what is next, it is waiting, not knowing it has been found. He removes his coat, because this is his favorite part and he wants to feel all of it. This is freedom and this is the price, he wants to know if I still dream of Love's touches. My Love is coming, I can see her hands, they are gently closing, I am returning, the distance is quieting like light, the distance between where I am and where I must be is no longer spreading.

I believe in Love's pursuit. It allows me to finally see the reality the Stranger speaks of, as he wipes it from his mouth. He laughs at the tremble of a lover's embrace. He laughs at the wishes they believe always hide in the dark. 'Wishes are most horrible in the light,' he says. It is a demand and not an invitation, to clearly see what Love and I will never forget. He challenges me to find a piece he did not touch. This is the result, when freedom embraces the untouchable. When the world intrudes where it does not belong.

I am more horrible than I ever imagined. I have one leg in and through the chair, it is long behind me, some ten paces or more, with a useless foot turned upside down and walking on the wall. The other stretches before me, its knee is bent up through the table and back down again, it has gone through the floor, I feel the tips of my toes brushing across the tracks. My enormous head is misshaped, my useless mouth has slid to the side of my face, my nose has escaped from between my eyes. I can watch purple ripples racing up and down my back, I can see my shoulders and the long arms they spill. He has taken all but a trace from me, and it is a trace I can not find.

The Stranger tells me Love is coming, she is coming to find my sweet face. The first kiss will be delicious, the second will be his, and the third will be forever. It is the thing of dreams. He tells me no love can be so blind, but yes, yes we will beg for blindness, and he will already be gone. He has granted enough wishes, he has granted enough chokes.

I am a nightmare, and not even Love will have me now. He tells me I should be kept in a sack and hidden from children, there is not a sea or continent that would have me now. The Stranger and I both feel Love's pursuit, she is coming with an ache and a comfort. He says it was an absolute pleasure to give this to our eyes. I am a wreckage and a cruelty, there is a sickness everywhere but within my soul. He is curious, he wonders if she will see it. The one stone he chose not to lift. Our love was never meant to be tested, but will she scream into the clouds. The Stranger smiles, he will present me as the man long taken, the man ill taken, the man who truly needed nothing and then suffered want. It was a want I was given, a want I wear like the skin of a chain.

'And the bride,' he says, the charging bride, he waits to see my face when I can not hide from her reaction. True love is a closeness unspoken. The Stranger offers a closeness only shadows know. He wants her to bring her feet and bring her hands, he is already twice fat with humanity, he knows our limits and knows our fears, and he wonders if we feel the touch of forever more than his touch. He wonders if we will see forever beyond what he leaves upon our eyes.

I sprawl heavy across the room he lifted twice for us, the room he dropped twice for us. Once for me and once for her reckless pursuit. My eyes are kneeling and my ears long not to hear. The Stranger assures me she is coming, and when she arrives, I will know. He will already be gone, but he will hear the cry. He will always be the twist in the prayer. His centuries are older than ours, his dances need no music. He will never suffer the devotion of a mother's kiss or the devotion of an infant's hands. He walks with a freedom no heart can endure. The end is coming, faster and hotter than trust, he assures me. He would give my last years to watch Love find me.

I would not stop Love's pursuit, even if I could. No matter the state in which she finds me. We have been lost and waiting and found before. I want her to crush through the doors, and I hope she remembers the hands that once held her. I want her pursuit though we may not survive. The Stranger laughs and laughs. Hands can drop and never return, hands can release and never forgive. He has never known the minute we share before midnight, the moment I kiss her heart, he has never known our minute after midnight. He has known only the slow drowning crawl he has given us. He has never found the places our faces have been. He spits on the floor and walks in it.

The Stranger threatens my eyes when I tell him his lies can not hold the truth. Love has arms he can not count and they are coming, and I believe in her pursuit. My enormous head falls backwards, it rests on my spine. I will wait for tomorrow, or the next, as I ooze and consume this room. I hear footsteps coming, and I know she is coming, and there is nothing the Stranger or the strangers or the world can do to slow them. He walks up and across my chest. But I am creating a space for an angel, she is singing a song I can hear. The pursuit is relentless and my mouth is open. I close my eyes, and the strangers are using tools. I close my eyes, and they are using fantasy and doubt. I hang onto a memory in this troubled, troubled room.

I feel delicious, spread across a chopping block. I hear the galloping pursuit. I am happy in this place of no happiness. My Love will find me in any dark turn, in any damp light. I can feel myself crawling, but I have already chosen, here in a place where there are no choices. There is a truth I can not accept. I hear laughter, and I don't know if it is mine or theirs. My next breath comes with a heave. The Stranger has spoken enough, there is mud in my veins now. I am Johnny Industry, and a light has entered the madness, I see the chains across the floor and I see them climbing the walls.

The Stranger exited like a thought and now returns like a sick slow drip. It will be tomorrow, or the next, as you say, he says. Because it has no meaning. Love and I were like birds falling from a nest. We were a game he did not need to play. But even strength can find panic. We have seen what we were never meant to see. He shrugs his long shoulders, he walks where he wishes and his tricks trespass the holes. Love is the brightest light I have ever known, and he has me sitting in the darkness, regretting every feeling I allowed him to know.

The Stranger sits with his knees high at his chest, he sits like mischief. It was too simple, to roll in like a cloud, to change want to need. He had his fingers inside, stirring and swimming. And he licks them, telling me I lost all I had for something he created. He has taken us to where our steps can't unwalk and our eyes can't uncurl. I have unlearned many things in his hands.

'I may keep you one more day, but I have been gone for seven,' the Stranger says. He speaks only to feel the softness. He speaks only to gauge my loss. But he tells me not to worry, she will find every piece of me he has left. The manner in which he steals and returns is the reason the world has a crooked face. This will all be over soon, all I have to do is be present. The ropes will drop from the ceiling and the wheels will drag me into the sunlight. I will have no choice but to be present.

He does not care if I believe he has stolen a year or a minute from her arms. Love is coming and her pursuit is no secret, and I have dreamed, and that is no secret, either. Nothing is hidden from the Stranger. He tells me that perhaps if we had not loved so lavishly and loved as though no one were watching or listening, he may have walked unseen and unheard past our lives. But Love and I, we have the devotion only children and angels know. He could not walk past such wild promises without stopping. The gods and the universe had us dripping with cream, and he had to stop to spoil the sweetness.

Love is my force, and he would pity her if he were capable of feeling such things, but he does not like touching such things with his hands. Treachery was his only option, otherwise we would be hanging from his clothes. Love is coming, and he is allowing time to cave and bend to her want. The Stranger wants me to know, he conceded nothing, it was finished after he was satisfied. He will not forget us, and we will live to forget him. He never keeps his promises and he promises we will worry about the return of his touch. He will disappear from us, for the final time tonight, and silence will occupy the space his voice leaves behind. And now beyond the silence, the breathing is growing, the sounds of the train, the distance, and the fury of the pursuit. She is coming to steal the unstolen, and I love her even more. She follows me to where I never went.

INSECT

I never burdened the insect inside me with a name, the one the Stranger never found. It walks with my taken legs, it is in my ears when I appear not to hear. It is in my mouth like a last flame, it is upon my tongue like the words he never took. It climbs behind my eyes and holds a warm photograph. It is in me, searching, it climbs and clumsily flies, it hides and it heals. It races from shoulder to shoulder, I feel it in my back, and it asks why, why, and it roots about, beneath my scalp, it offers to nest and lay eggs.

There is an insect inside me that pushes the cough from my throat when I am unable to see. It is a chill to prevent the cold, it is stirring within to tell me I am not alone. I feel its tickle traveling miles and miles. It leaves no taste and it leaves no sting, it leaves no webs and it leaves no worry. It is just beneath my skin and it swims in my blood. It shares my thoughts and it shares these shadows. It tells me I am a man hopelessly and thoughtlessly in love. There are moments the bones know what they know.

I make no move to capture it, I make no move to startle it. I would like to see its wings, I would like to count its tiny legs. I would like to touch its smooth hard shell I have felt rub against my bones. I would like to speak to it. I don't want to scare it away. To feel it is to be human, to allow it is to be more. The insect inside me, that perseveres, the one the Stranger never found.

There is an insect inside me that might remember the smooth fires Love and I knew in the night. I want it to know I am begging, I want it to find the courage to emerge. The Stranger is gone and will not return, maybe not for hours, maybe not for days. There is nothing and no one to harm it, as it cleanses my insides. Don't be afraid to come out, I feel Love's cooling kisses across my arms and my chest. Don't be afraid of the light, the Stranger is gone and the darkness isn't returning. He has his prize and I still feel her eyes. The insect inside me is listening, it is rising, it is climbing.

It is coming and I am waiting and shivering. It is in my throat and has me like want. Its wings are finally behind my teeth, I smile and it grabs my tongue. There is nothing more to say. It comes across what was my cheek and ventures towards what was my eye. I look upon it like an old mirror, and see what I was and not what I have become. It has a face I know, it falls like a slow thick tear drop, it has the color of warm and ease.

The insect that is now a teardrop, it pulls from the place in my heart the Stranger never found. This is closer to forever the eternal Stranger will ever know. I sense it deliciously, it is more like love than mud, lighter than the lightest mist. I picture it dropping onto Love's forehead. The world has stopped spinning, we sense it, the three of us. It hovers quieter than a never whisper. The teardrop lingers just above her eyes, it wants to feel before it is felt. It wants to waste in forever, it wants to glow in forever. A teardrop with the freedom rain will never know, a single teardrop that will never be heard. It wills itself to be remembered. It finds Love's cheek as though it belongs there, as though it will dance there. A lone teardrop that urges an angel to return to a human night.

There is no weight and no fall, no capture and no doubt, the teardrop can fly just as it can crawl. The teardrop remembers before it became an insect. It was a memory. A memory of a first anxious and hungry kiss that tore the centuries into pieces. A kiss that redressed the night and renamed it. The teardrop uses its hands and reunites us again. It leads Love and I down a path, to step away from the desire so we may feel the devour. It leads us past Thursday and Friday and just over and around Love's chin, it drips down her neck spread like countless days. It wanders to her shoulders and finds her arms all the way down to her hands. The teardrop drips to her hip, wanting to be noticed, it hides in a curve, wanting to be found. It rolls down through the weeks and the months, it rolls down through the invitations, it travels her legs down to her toes. The insect that became a teardrop that was once a memory and now a fire I follow.

Forever is as simple as the touches we feel without a word or a glance. Forever is the wet in the night, the unbearable separation of sleeping, it is the children that grew into lovers in our hearts. Forever is the leap together into the impossible divide. Forever is today and tomorrow, it lays comfortably within an hour, it will never leave and never be asked. Forever is the pull and the calm.

It is in her hands as they tell my face how many times she has loved me. Forever can not harm and can never be healed.

Forever is irresistible and can not be counted. Love and I can not be saved and it is awful. And the way my hands answer and tell her face how many times I have loved her. That is what keeps the monsters at bay.

I want to find my feet upon the world beneath me. I want to find the air it is filled with. I want to live our promise. I want to remember the thousands of kisses I have given Love, and I want to tell her how I will give her the first.

The Stranger has returned as though he never left. He sits as though he was invited. A corner of the room has formed around him, as if to give him a place. 'Love never conquered the world,' he says. He has given us the collapse and yet here we are, beneath it and within it, struggling to find a kiss. He gives an exaggerated yawn. Yes, Love is coming, and she is late. He has tasted the time and asks if I believe he will simply give it back. He knew I would try to dream. I risked everything and all, just to realize the light is nothing against the heaviness. The teardrop wandered across Love and I savored it, inch by inch, and the sweat rolling across the back of my neck was the price and it was worth it.

The Stranger tells me I asked for freedom, and that is what he granted, by his own definition. He speaks without mercy or remorse. He has made me the cage, and I am the first animal held within it. I am the clearest deception, I am the unforgiveable lie. And yet still I believe, before I was and after I have become Johnny Industry, Love and I will share a kiss the moon has never seen. Love is coming and the Stranger has taken the rest. With two fingers he plucks the insect from where it hides.

THE UNVEILING

There is a voice against the side of my head. The inevitable is awake, now, Johnny, it is outside and no one can see it. The Stranger's train is coming to a cease, not a stop. Its grinding arrival comes without a whistle, it is a screeching complaint. The train appears through a wall of fog, it appears straight and true like a conflict with the sunlit morning, it emerges like a gesture, the noise hangs like a warning. This is the final take. This is nothing like surrender, it has already come to be.

'You can close your eyes one more time, Johnny, and it doesn't matter if you ever open them again,' he says. I find him sitting on the opposite side of the room from where I heard his voice. I haven't the strength. He waits until he is recognized. The insect is quiet and still beneath his boot, and he scrapes me from the heels. He tells me with slow words, he has given me my own voice back. Because the work is finished. He tells me Love is nearly here, she is so close.

The Stranger shows me the hat he will wear today. He is going to walk through the crowd and brush shoulders, he is going to smile and shake hands, because he has already disappeared. He puts on the hat and is immediately unrecognizable, wearing this face I will never forget. The Stranger demands I scream his name. I can't remember it. I saw it once in the distance, somewhere before yesterday. He tells me I was the slightest of weights, I was no burden. He would knocked me aside as he would a feather of a dead bird, had it not been for her. I am fortunate to stand beside Love. I can trust his opinion, for he deals only in fortune and misfortune. My greatest failure was to attempt to stand tall. It does not matter whether the wish was mine, it was the wish he granted.

At first I believe it is his hands, but no, I can feel it in my mouth, and I say it aloud. 'None of this was real.' The Stranger assures me he will linger. It is his price, to be the stink in my sweetest touch. Love and I lived impossible dreams, and such dreams ache through his tongue and he finds them unbearable and he can not help but stop and touch. His eyes like to feel them sag and ruin, and he carries them in his pockets. For a time.

The Stranger tells me he could have squeezed through but an inch. But I stepped away from the safety of the quiet, and I gave him a moment. I fell, and I fell into the machine, I became the machine. It was a slash to the guts, it was a wrenching twist, it was his perfect idea. He scratched his signature with a fingernail, and no one will ever see. I glance down for relief, I can't be burdened by his stare any longer. My hands are still being devoured by the machine.

'No, no, Johnny, it is much simpler than that,' he says. My horrible fingers have been in the eyes of thousands, countless thousands, and my gruesome mouth has been soft in their ears. He tells me to look out the window he has given again. He tells me to stare through the glass without seeing myself. He asks what I see, and I say I see people. There is a crowd, a crush of humanity, some arrived before dawn. They press together in fascination, they were pressed to come and they don't understand why. They raced their neighbors here, they elbow their neighbors here. They fight for a place they don't belong. They strain for something I will never give them.

The Stranger stands and grinds a final step into the insect. I am Johnny Industry, we are Johnny Industry. He created me, and he will flick me from the brim of his hat. I am a brief splash that wasted into a phenomenon that soared like a comet. I am the crash they are all about to witness. I am already burning. And none who are outside know why they formed into a crowd, and none will remember. They can't feel the chains about their arms and the chains around their ankles. They won't understand why they wished to embrace me, but I, I will never forget.

Love is coming, yes, she is relentlessly pursuing, to find the pieces he leaves. He tells me there was a moment, and that was when I was taken, I refused to lose all I had. I know he speaks no truths, he tells me he possesses what I will never surrender. He tells me a man with dreams has nothing at all. A man with a coat can be left in the cold, a man with a plate can be left in hunger. He dissected me, in a moment's hesitation.

The Stranger recklessly created a mystery and a man, he gave me many faces but only one name. The goal was the end, the end is the achievement. The crowd will be more than disappointed, the crowd will forget. And what becomes of Love and I. It is rare that two may suffer his pleasure. It is rare that two become too wide for his gaze. His hands did their work, he will leave us to the night. When he exits this train and his steps strike the ground, he could be in the next state or town, or last year or tomorrow. It is the beauty of being lost to all, known by none, and remembered by few.

'You will remember me, Johnny,' he says. I was the narrator who became the writer who could not speak to his Love. And even the long painful fall down the hill will not return me to where I was. With his will, by his will. I was a book, a song, a movie, I was a phrase, I was pepper in the senses, I was a wrinkle in the senseless. I was never meant to be part of history. I dared out of the comfortable soil. I found the misery that was beyond my reach. The Stranger tells me, home is a soft disgusting place he finds intolerable and painful to the touch, and I should have never left. The shreds that remain are his pleasure.

The Stranger shrugs, he starts to leave and now pauses, he smiles and bows. He is a prince to no one, he is a price to all, he has only the power to unfold and to unshuffle. He has nothing to offer and sees everything he might take. He wants to whisper too late into my ears. I never asked for any of this, and he is certain I will never ask again. He is leaving, but one day he will be the rain on the rooftop, and a question before we sleep. He tells me Love is beautiful, and she is too late. She will miss the big finish, a last dance that will famously last but a few moments and bring the misery of fame. He tells me he will keep only one promise, and that is why my skin is crawling so maddeningly.

He leaves me to the people outside, and he calls them mine. I can hear their impatience. They are drawn to me, he has tethered them to me, their eyes are blinded and about to see, their minds have been pulled and pummeled to the brink of fascination. Their mouths are confused and waiting to whistle and cheer. With his promise kept, the long thick ropes are falling from the ceiling. The room is filled with activity and bodies and hands. Heavy ropes loop around my knees, my feet, they are beneath my arms, across my chest and the table. There is a heave and a failed lift. The ropes tighten around the machine and tighten close under my chin, there is a heave and I am dropped.

There are louder voices and I am finally lifted from the floor. The ropes bite tighter, I rise a little higher, and a wheeled platform is slid beneath me. They remember the Stranger said to let me fall, this will be the most brief fall, the painless fall before the exquisite fall. There is a thickening thump in a heap, it is me, and the table.

The side of the train is slowly opening, daylight finds the first inches and becomes hungry for the room and perhaps hungry for me. The Stranger is whispering at my side, I look for him, he stands, waiting for the wall to raise. He told me he would only speak the truth once. He vanished forever and returned. He vanished and never left. Not before seeing my reaction. The Stranger is already gone, and I know it, he is gone and I will never forget.

The daylight reaches my eyes and it is blinding. I feel the platform wheeled forward, teasing at first, and now moving generously. There is a hum and a harm, a commotion, a conversation washing through the crowd. For a moment it lingers, and I nearly forget where I am and what I am. A silence grows and it slices, through the sidewalk, through the streets, through the barriers, through the crowd my eyes have yet to see. I feel them, as a silence lays upon their hats and their shoulders, it dirties their best dresses and their finest pants. I feel as they shift from one uncomfortable foot to another. I feel the Stranger and his absence he promised.

This could be the birth of time, with no sound, no breath, no movement. Before the innocence, before the violence. Silence, and then a groan that seems to come from beneath the ground and rise through the crowd. And anguish, human anguish, it comes in waves and it comes for me. A woman's shriek, and now women shrieking, and men crying out aloud, startled and forgetting their confidence, and children calling for their parents, and parents sobbing and fleeing, and dogs, sobbing, howling and fleeing.

It may have lasted an excruciating minute, it could have been two. My smashed Jacko lantern face and my monstrous presence. It has traveled the world and left me to sit in this silence. The crowd is gone, and its absence is pungent. The quiet of the day is fighting to come. The streets are not empty, it is much worse and much heavier. There is nobody here. The cries are gone and the wind is blowing. This is the ice I own, this is the strange beyond the could and the want. I am going to just sit here. The Stranger once told me in a darkness, he wrapped it around my shoulders before he wrapped his words around my neck. My face would travel the world in fifteen seconds, and if there were any mercy, it would be forgotten.

I am at the edge, and waiting for the grace and understanding we are told awaits. I am laying in its fingers. The narrator who would have been a writer is gone, his face and his name are gone. And I have spoken not a single word. The Stranger stirred the reaction and exited before he tasted a spoon of the soup. I am the horror that became, the dogs don't return to sniff at me, sit and wait for the rats that don't appear. I shudder into a sob, for all the time and spaces Love and I have lost. The time and the spaces I can not reconcile, not with her, not with him, not with the devil or a crowd of angels. With legs I might carry myself towards the memories of home. With legs I might carry myself to lay between the tracks and the train. Even the morning refuses to come closer to me.

In the sunlight I feel the loss before me, it is coming for me, and I feel the heat of the fire from behind. The train is burning and so is all that transpired, it is burning down to the tracks. All who were inside have left, just as the Stranger, just as the crowd. My hands slip free from the machine. It belongs in the fire but I haven't the strength to lift it. Perhaps Johnny Industry belongs to the fire but it refuses to approach me. The fire slowly retreats, I realize I am now free from the name and all the faces. I am left to pretend to be the man I was.

All the worst of me remains. These terribly long arms too stretched and too weak to lift what were my hands. These legs are now gnarled timbers, they are beneath me and beside me, in front of me and behind me. What places we may have gone, what places they may have taken me. My back can not straighten with the weight of my head at one end. There is but the dying heat of the fire and the silence of a morning's refusal. My eyes, these eyes, laugh at the thought of relief. These eyes speak more now than this mouth.

I am sitting within my own long low moan. I would ask forgiveness, for every second lost. There is no forgiveness coming. Forgiveness was the first to abandon the hunt, followed by reason. These thoughts seem to come from a wind I can't see, or perhaps from the shadow of the fire now quenched. Now there is only freedom. The narrator is gone, the man is gone, the insect is gone, and Johnny Industry is gone.

'There will never be a lover so true to take what remains of you.' Where these two empty streets join in a corner, there is a solitary lamp post with a solitary figure leaning against it. The Stranger smiles and speaks his last lie. He has told me he speaks only in lies. I will not remember all of them but will feel their feathers and oils. He vanishes forever, time and again, and returns as he wishes. He would never dream of missing the reunion. It is going to be a pleasure that twists his hands in his pockets. The fitful and fraught lovers' reunion he will wear like candy around his neck.

The Stranger tells me he is elbow deep into the next offering, but he wanted to see how handsome I was, laying in abandonment. He wishes I would say my old name, so he can feel the thorns. There is no where to walk and no where to burn. This is lasting and cold and turning red. His eyes never close and he can see how thick I am wearing the doubts. He promises to never disappear, now that I have fed from his hands and fed from his madness. I feel his words and his lips on the skin of my ear and the back of my neck. He asks how true is my truth, and then screams the most horrifying scream.

SHADE

Love appears through a shade of question and a shade of darkness we were never to have known. She kisses me perfect and the red goes to purple, and sinks to blue and then to pink. She waits for me to take another first breath. And if I am finally seeing what is true, she has found me. She has found me in an unmoving sprawl across the pavement, she has found me in these horrible pieces. With these arms that haven't the strength to hold and these legs that have lost the warmth of walk. I wonder, is this another peace or another dungeon. My Leo. Love dips and lowers slow through the only hole she can find to reach me, and that hole is another kiss. The shade of disbelief becomes a shade of anxious. Don't sleep now, I rise into a shade of comfort.

I can not feel if my eyes are truly opened and my ears are hearing her breaths. Yes, my Leo, this is real, we are real. I was never going to find my way through the Stranger's cloud, and she is bringing me to the shade just outside. I can't explain where I have been, I can't explain what I have become. Love is here like a promise we never had to speak, a promise we never had to hear.

How utterly gruesome I must appear to her, as she looks upon me with the eyes I remember. I want her to see me as I was before yesterday, before some of my fingers were surrendered to the machine, before irretrievable time was surrendered to the machine. I question my own eyes as she does not recoil, she smiles sweetly and has thankful tears. She looks through the shade and sees memories within the monster they created. She does not see the pieces, she does not see the chains the Stranger left as reminders. He left one in my stomach and one across my back, and he promised, when I don't hear his voice, I will hear them shake and shift, I will hear them call.

I find the shade of Love's words. I look tired and hungry, but I am with her again. We are in the shade of dancing laughing fingers. There is no lovers' remorse, there is no lovers' plague. Love speaks in a midnight kiss against today. Every word she speaks has the bite of a cure, every word she speaks has the bite of a warm heal. We are in the shade of the known against the unknown. There is the chilling feel of the air becoming too close, as though it is searching for what he created. But there is no room for the three of us, Love takes my hand.

'It has been the longest three days,' she says. I hold onto her desperately, to save myself from the shade of the heaviest crumble, the cruelest deception, and the long unraveling. The Stranger took everything, and he took time, he took days and weeks, and I consumed it all. He fed me with his longest fingers down my throat. Love begins to pull me from beneath the piles the he laid me beneath. I surrendered everything, that first night. I was lost the moment she drove away, I was lost the moment I boarded his train. I am grateful she burned it to the ground.

When I boarded the train, his hands appeared to swallow my shoulders. It was to be five days, we agreed. And when I wasn't listening, he told Love he would be finished in three. I would be broken in three. She could try to find and manage the pieces in three. How quickly he must have worked, how frantically he must have worked, knowing what Love would become. It was hidden in the phrases he chose to use with her, with words like delighted and enchanted and pleasure. I am in the shade she must now rescue me from. She tells me what day it is, and she has never told me a lie. This is the weight of birth and death and truth all at once upon unprepared shoulders. I am sick in the gutter and his grueling laugh reappears. He reminds me, he took me places I could only have gone alone, he stole from me and refashioned and reinvented me, when I was alone. The shade of one is hollow and helpless, the shade of two is forever.

What could not be and what never happened is pressing hard against my face, I am trying to pull at it with my hands. My breath is out of my chest. She left me at a train, she left me in a ditch, she left me at an airport. She returned to the building with the clocktower standing in front of it. And I was no where to be found. The Stranger bent the light. His work was complete before I arrived.

Love searched to find me, because she could not see my face in the face I was given, and she could not hear my voice in any word I spoke. I was not telling our story, and she did not come to make me remember. I am not unraveled and I am not unwound. This is the shade of never forgotten and never gone, of never now and always forever. She is speaking against the howl in the distance, she is speaking over the howl in the distance. She is speaking over the ringing bells. We will never lose what I never lost.

She has an angel's shade coming from her lips, and I remember the little innocent devilry in her steps. I remember what it is to stand, I remember what it is to be free and walk. We met before the crushing shade of centuries, we met in a burning flash and could do nothing but know and be. Love tells me it is time to go home, and there is no need to forgive the missing hours and the missing days. This is all and everything in her smiling eyes, and yes, I want to go home.

The shadow of Johnny Industry does not follow us, it lays on the ground where the crowds once cheered and wept. It lays flat and unrecognizable, it speaks no words. His spread had no harm, with his filth and his fury. Love and I walk with no light coming between our hands, I am not the narrator or the writer, I am not sung or hung by that name. I am Leo and I am hers, and there is an endless night approaching. I have been returned to the shade of the cherished, I have returned from the miles and miles I never traveled. I am pulled to safety from those who never captured me. I have become what never changed. Now it is us and ours, that bring the whispers to my neck, it is Love and I, hot and up at my eyes. And the shade came come with all its shapes and dreams, Love and I are going home.

The door asks no questions as I enter as though I never left, the walls don't creak disapproval. I find my face next to hers. There is the sweet strange burden of adoration, and its slow careless burn jumps me right back into the boil. I move her hair aside to kiss her shoulder. That one is for tonight. There is no shade to be walked away from, there is no shade that can not be brought to its knees. I move her hair again, to kiss her other shoulder. That one is for tomorrow. I might be a little discolored, and maybe not everything will be forgotten.

The night seems to have a promise of no mischief, so I remove the tatters and the rest of my clothes. Love is here, in a never wait, and in a never left, I want to come with a kiss that never disappoints. There is a shade of knowing that reaches beyond any shade of becoming. There is a shade of glory that can't be wrestled, it can't fall to an army, it can't pale before doubt. There are some hours that can't be wrecked into empty, these are the hours that run like a stew, they sleep like a beast, they cover like a warm comfort.

My legs tell me I am home, and this peace tells me I belong. I lay here, thick, taller than the bed. I hope tonight lays upon the roof to keep me inside. I wanted to give her everything, and Love opens her arms and tells me we are here, and tells me I belong to it now, this is the first place and the first moment I ever needed to be. This is the shade of the tumbling ache with the motionless whispers.

Our steps into forever will never be unfelt or unheard. We are in a motionless light, in a motionless night, only our hearts are moving. I am so far from his voice and so far from the gnawing fame, I am so far from the grinning loss and the troubles of the darkness. The dreams have docked their boats, they have uncasted their lines, if I could feel closer than this, I would drown in it. Love eases in beside me and becomes the blossom and the petals, she becomes the rise and the fall, and the truth I can not untouch. And maybe I did not breathe before the curving shade of this moment, and maybe I did not want to.

Our lovers' time holds everything else beyond the silent windows, our lovers' time ignores the knocking at the doors. There is a softness that can not be changed or turned inside out. There is a softness that falls over us like a heat. Love rises above rest and above sleep, she is up on her arms, and she tells me I am home and the shade has been banished from the pillows, it has been banished to crawl all night on all fours.

My eyes tell her I can no longer feel or see the train or its tracks. There remains the hint of the burn, as everything recovers and returns from his to theirs to ours. She has regrown from a dream to a partner to a lover. I am once again in her web, we have found my arms and legs, and I am no where near starving, I can not find it. She feels my eyes and finds them and I swallow. Her charms are a brace I need, for confidence, for recovery. She has my eyes and tells me they are coming out of the shade, and I tell her I need nothing more than the long cling of tonight and the longer cling of tomorrow.

She sees him in my eyes, the Stranger who never was and could not speak, she sees me fighting the fight I can not have. The shade that dragged hope into fear and loss. Wounds will heal when the wounds disappear and scratch no more. I turn into her hands and turn away from his voice. The creak and the call of this lavish night, Love has me by the shoulders and will not let my bones fall. She is a grasp at my lips, I am her man, I am hers. The Stranger is fading, he is out there, he is a sour in a kiss, a mallet brought to a thought.

Love tells me this is our night and we have never surrendered another. I am going to be taken by her gentle madness, I am going to be cast into it. This warmth is a paradise, the mouth I have is open, the steps I have are not chased. There is a shade in the corner of the room that will not be forgotten. It is a shiver and a crash, it is a voice in the peace. She wants me to remember, I am not a target or a prey, I am a hunger and a meal. In these hours between sleep and wake, my Love is deep and heavy against me, she is inside our bed and all around me. I am cautiously and quietly trying not to escape. I hold her tighter than I have held her before, and she hushes the storm, she has my face and my voice, and she hushes the outside to be still. Love has taken the feel from the temperature, she has chased the cries from the room. She has seen my face again and heard my voice again, and the Stranger wonders how I believe I will ever escape his. He comes in a lightning strike, in a cruel walk, a savage push. I was given the unforgiveable, the untouchable was stolen. I can not run and I can not hide. He says he will never stop whispering, I am a spent fire, a stomach with guts. I am his history, I am not a servant, I am his time. I cave into Love's arms, and will listen to her until the morning.

We are approaching the shade of midnight and will reach beyond it with these four hands. I wonder if she found me by cleverness or luck, but no, no she found me, one heart seeking another. She never wanted me to be more than I am, she never needed to hear more than I spoke. Love holds me, reclaimed, as the never taken, she fastens herself and the hooks within me. She tells me she will call me her darling one thousand times before she ever speaks his empty name.

Love is the space that surrounds me, and he is trying to take my hands from her whispers. He is trying to keep my voice from her fingers. I don't have to struggle to find her now. He kept me from her for one day. And now she is a shade of a kiss and a promise to keep me safe, even when he is just right there, sitting in the corner, waiting. I can't stretch beyond her arms now.

Love sleeps in a coil beside me, she sleeps in a roast beside me, she has her locks upon me, she has her freedom on me. I feel it in my thigh that crosses her hip, and I can't take the delicious fall he was giving me. He speaks with a stuttering static, his voice clicks like a hen, he could have made me more than a flash. I could have reached such heights with his lift. His hands that move mountains, and Love's hands find me again. The narrator who was to become a writer, was a flash faster than a blink. 'You are my everything, stay here with me, Leo,' Love says in her sleep. We are safe beyond the shade of the driving winds, and if I open my eyes, I will see it is the two of us, in a magnificent bed, in a magnificent life.

She breaks the sudden cool with a blanket drawn across my shoulders and back. She can place an ear to my heart and hear all the words I owe her. If I am going to be the narrator, I should kiss her as he did. If I am going to be someone else, I should kiss her with his passion. Because no one else was invited. My throat is hers and it will find the words, through the years. Love smiles in her sleep as though the years begin in this very moment. I count her words as though I count myself to sleep. And in a bright and shocking lunge, I am beyond a shade of the Stranger's madness, and I am in the colors of serenity.

I will sleep tonight beyond the weight of the greatest mistake I nearly asked. I will sleep in her endless arms and trust. And all the perfect words I will say to her chin and the tip of her nose and to the long comfort of her dreaming. I am in the depths I never had to seek, I am in the pleasure of an unnamed morning, somewhere between the royal blue she wears and the skin that awaits beneath it. I am in the steam and the silence no one else will ever know. I lay in the ashes that are a masterpiece, I lay in the coals before the genuine and the fire took their grip.

I can not escape the touch of all we pass, every moment is a linger, every moment is a longing. And nothing has and nothing possesses her sweet face. There is no feel to what I dreamed of before. There is only tomorrow and hello and again, and I love you. I can not walk untouched by the colors of the shade, and all that can never fade.

ALWAYS US, AT LAST

I haven't counted the days and nights since you brought me home, and I won't count those to come. We are carved into our bed, here between want and dreams. In the too quiet and comfortable, in the too full and necessary, we are nostalgic and hopeful. There will be many sleeps and wakes before you and I walk beyond forgiving our faces, forgetting his voices.

You are farther in that journey than I, judging by this trickling wait. I would love your lips today, I wouldn't mind a crawl slow down to the small of my back. I wait for your eyes to tell me it is morning. What was raw and torn is now a lingering scratch, a scratch with a sound that no longer closes the distance. We don't speak of him and he is not defeated, we are no longer in his arms. Those days were endured more than they are finished. Those nights still prowl and hunt.

I press against your elbow, and remember where I am. My teeth have renested, my face has returned to smile, my hands have regrown, my arms can be useful, my legs have reinvented their shape and their lines. There are no more shadows being left behind. The Stranger is too vain to be dismissed, I see him tapping a finger upon his chin, asking which of us was to forget and which of us was to forgive. He wonders if I truly deny the helplessness of fame and the thrill of captivity. He is coming into the bake, the loneliness is gathering.

The light beside the bed has been turned on, my thoughts have driven you awake. I don't mean to pull you from the warmth. 'Don't, Leo, we don't speak his name,' you say. Forgiveness is strength and contempt, forgetfulness is elusive. The illusions are gone, and I am home. I return to your eyes, I return to this feast. This is beyond love and adoration, this is salvation. You press close to me and provide sleep without anxious dreams. I know your breath will not leave my body again.

I am in the sweet turmoil of waiting. I wait for your magic, I wait for you to come outside and shock the gray. You pull it into a harmless tail of a cloud, and now it rests above, seeking nothing more. We whispered close and together last night, you told me I am not your task, you find me each day like a new wonder. You teach me patience, you teach me the silence when there is no chase. You teach me the small curiosities are more important than the answers.

You charge at me with your hands and dance today, and show my feet they will never forget their roots. There is no place in heaven for us, we are in the dirt and beyond the sky. I show you I have not forgotten your favorite touch, your favorite pleasure and direction. We have no boundaries. I have your secrets and you have mine. We are not stealing more time when we share another kiss, we are redressing the ones we have had and waking the ones we have missed. And if I could but find the words, and take your hand, there will be no hesitation felt before the depth.

There is nothing to forgive and nothing to forget. The first fire has no fear, the second has no burn, the third has no doubt. We are in the longest bend of the enduring and endearing curves. We are in the straight lines of the strongest winds. You fall over me and seep into me and call me by every name I will answer. 'My Leo.'

We are in the tenderness and the kneel, the release and the kindness of the forever things. They are the monsters, they are the collision, they are the hunger, they are the savages that broke free from the nets. They are beyond the more and the want. We are in the juice on their plates. They bring us into the silk, into the soft, they give us the reason and not the knowledge. The forever things scare away the chains and the charms, they lay across our eyes like visions we can't escape. They remind us we were only gently denied, we were guided away from the past and prevented from reaching the future. We learned to embrace their justice and their rewards fashioned into days and nights. I have loved only you, not since the beginning of time, but since we learned to see and walk as they do.

The forever things are a roar and a rage in our minds, they began on a day with no name, and continue relentlessly. You and I, my Love, we found each other heavier than the snow and more searching than the rain. We were the only two alive within those inches of the universe's memories. The forever things trusted me to know you and love you from afar, and closer and still closer you dared to approach. I knew and loved you before the innocence, before the roads were traveled and then unkept. We never lost the play and the way we fell. We were the matched stars that learned to speak, we were the patience and endurance that could not be taught. And now the forever things choose to magnify what could never be lost. We were in love the day hunger lost its feet. We were in love the day perfection lost its touch.

The forever things bring the excruciating nights, the pounding and pounding days. I remember each time we escaped, I remember each time we loved in sunlight and loved in shadow. I remember when we stole away, hand in hand, before they taught us the dances, before they showed us how to sing. The forever things bring you across my skin in breaths and hairs and lay me across your mouth. They bring you to me with arms and legs and

I try to speak through the river. Give me your eyes when you can stand not one more kiss, give me your neck when your eyes can stand no more. I have burned all my bravery and all my questions. I will follow you now and always, through the opened door and down the path.

There are bones beneath my meat and bones within my soul, they rattle and ache, but they will never roam. I'll decline the invitations of saints and kings, I'll decline those of the wisest and richest. I'll refuse the tempt of the world and the moon and the sun, just to have one more night of peace with you. You are my enchanting force, the seas will dream before they can dream so, you are a rise the mountains will fail to reach. You are a truth and a beauty untouched.

A wind can not find me without your fingers. My heart knows only a forever and a longing so simple and sweet. There is an old want, an old dream, wetted by rains that came to be. We loved before freedom, we loved before the denial, we loved before the universe fell asleep and laid on its face. We loved before we were blind and deaf, and we learned nothing and suffered nothing. We were sung the melodies of mortals and fences. I don't want to return to the stars, I don't want to wait for chance again.

You wear my ring, and I wear the heavy brow of the narrator. I feel the words I might have sought, they are sliding down, leaving the back of my throat. We are bound by more that can be spoken, we are delivered by more that can be read. For 500 swollen years I have chased you, held you, been fed by you, lost you, found you. I can't speak words like eternity, or light, or cold. I speak words such as us. Us.

I can't learn another language to explain the lace and the soil, I can't create the words to paint the dream where I belong.

You have made me a man too large for my soul, who knows nothing as small as always. Love is the closest thing I know to the tremble within the fierce wings of an angel. And perhaps the magical end of our story was the beginning, and the last taste was the first.

You found me when we were never lost. You are a longing that knows no difference between day and night. My steps know no slow or pace, they are with yours, because there is no distance between here and forever. There is no reach or home beyond these hearts.

I walked into a garden, without a hint of a stay. I explored without a touch until my eyes could see. I found the most amazing and delicate and breathtaking sight. And having no urge to capture you or make you my own, I laid beneath you and felt myself growing.

We are never in the dark without closeness and warmth, we are never in the pale beyond the burn. We are never alone and never apart. There was a purpose and there never was a mystery. A single word was salvaged and remembered from each century, as they passed to endure the next. I want a kiss for each one you read. I want five kisses for five words.

I love you more now.

Made in United States
Cleveland, OH
06 October 2025

21171920R00075